THE GUNSMITH

477

Sheriff Iron Horse

Books by J.R. Roberts
(Robert J. Randisi)

The Gunsmith series

Gunsmith Giant series

Lady Gunsmith series

Angel Eyes series

Tracker series

Mountain Jack Pike series

COMING SOON!
The Gunsmith
478 – The Red Lady of San Francisco

For more information visit:
www.SpeakingVolumes.us

THE GUNSMITH

477

Sheriff Iron Horse

J. R. Roberts

SPEAKING VOLUMES, LLC
NAPLES, FLORIDA
2022

Sheriff Iron Horse

ISBN 978-1-64540-752-2

Chapter One

Hellcat, Texas

Sheriff Iron Horse poured himself a cup of coffee and set the pot back on the potbelly stove in his office. He carried the cup to the window and looked out at the main street of Hellcat, Texas. A fairly new town, expanding slowly, it contained all the though elements of a growing town. So brutal, in fact, that no one wanted the job of sheriff. Most of the men in Hellcat would rather break the law than enforce it.

Sammy Iron Horse was an Apache who had gone east to be educated, then came back west to put his education to work for his people. But his people didn't accept him and his new ways. Soon he found that the citizens in town didn't want anything to do with him, either. But since the job of town sheriff was available, he decided to volunteer for it. Wearing a badge, everyone would have to deal with him, the townspeople and his own tribe.

The mayor of Hellcat was dubious about hiring Iron Horse, but the town had gone too long without a lawman and the Apache promised to turn the tide in town, bringing to it law and order.

Six months in he had done his job. The mayor was very satisfied with his performance, while others had mixed feelings. The town's businessmen and storekeepers appreciated the order he had brought to things, while others—the lawbreakers and offenders who remained in town—plotted against him behind his back.

In the past three weeks there had been half a dozen attempts on Iron Horse's life, ranging from bushwhackings to a bold try one night while making his rounds. But Iron Horse had luck on his side and had killed the two men who had attacked him in the dark with knives.

For six months Sheriff Iron Horse had gone about his duties without the aid of a deputy. No one wanted that job any more than they'd wanted the sheriff's position. That was why he had sent for outside help. He expected the arrival of his friend—and deputy-to-be—any day now. So he continued watching the street from the window while drinking his morning coffee.

But this morning he didn't see anyone arriving in town, except the man walking toward his office. He left the window and sat behind his desk, because he thought it gave him an advantage.

The door opened and Mayor Ted Dandridge entered. He was tall, thin, in his fifties. He had been the mayor of Hellcat for six years. During that time, he had unsuccessfully lobbied for a change in the town's name. He thought the name, as it was, invited lawbreakers and troublemakers.

"No sign of your deputy yet?" the mayor asked.

"No."

"But he *is* coming, right?"

"Yes."

The mayor looked at the cellblock door.

"Any guests?"

"None."

"I'm always amazed at how many questions you can answer with a single word. You mind if I sit?"

"Please."

The mayor sat.

"Look," the man said, "you've been on the job six months, and done fine. But there are those in town who wish you'd dress more . . . white. You know, cut your hair, get rid of the bandana."

"No," Iron Horse said. "What else?"

"Are you giving any thought to stepping down? I mean, in light of the fact that somebody seems to want to kill you?"

"No," Iron Horse said. "I don't think stepping down would change that. Anything else?"

The mayor heaved a frustrated sigh.

Iron Horse had the feeling that his time behind the badge might be coming to an end.

"That's all," Mayor Dandridge said, rising. "Just let me know when your deputy gets here."

"Sure."

"And watch your back."

"Always."

The mayor left, and Iron Horse poured himself another cup of coffee.

***

Iron Horse's would-be-deputy approached town on horseback. He knew Hellcat was a small but growing town. He reined in and sat for a moment, regarding the town from a short distance. Iron Horse's telegram asking him to come and help was something he could not ignore. Sammy Iron Horse was a longtime friend and wouldn't be asking for help unless he really needed it.

He shook his horse's reins, dug his heels in, and started forward. The horse had only gone a few feet when there was a shot. The man heard it, then felt the bullet dig into his back like a hot poker. One thought passed through his mind as he fell to the ground.

Iron Horse was about to need a new deputy.

Chapter Two

Iron Horse turned as the door to the undertaker's office opened and the mayor stepped in.

"What happened?" the man asked.

Iron Horse pointed to the man on the table.

"This is—was—Charlie White Horse. We grew up together. I asked him to come and be my deputy and he agreed. Looks like somebody knew I sent that telegram and was waiting just outside of town to bushwhack him."

"How was he killed?"

"Backshot."

"A single shot?"

"Yes," Iron Horse said, "and well placed."

"What will you do now?"

"What else?" Iron Horse said. "Keep doing my job."

"What will you do about a deputy? Or, at least, someone to watch your back?"

"I don't know," Iron Horse said. "I don't believe I can trust anyone in this town."

"Then maybe you should step away," the mayor said. "You've done a fine job, but I don't want you to get killed for it."

"I don't intend to."

"Intend to what?"

"Step away, or get killed," Iron Horse said, "Like I told you this morning, I'm going to keep doing my job. Unless you fire me."

"I'm not firing you," the mayor said.

"Then I'll get to it."

"What are you going to do?"

"Find out who killed my friend, Charlie White Horse."

Iron Horse left the undertaker's office, having already arranged for White Horse's burial.

***

Iron Horse went back to his office, grabbed his coffee cup, sat behind his desk and poured whiskey instead of coffee. He drank it down and poured another. White Horse was his oldest friend. Now he was dead, because Iron Horse had asked him for help. He was supposed to keep Iron Horse from being killed. Now the Apache Sheriff had to find out who killed his friend.

He put the bottle of whiskey away. His first stop was going to be the telegraph office.

***

It was some indication that Hellcat was a town planning to grow that it had a telegraph office. Iron Horse entered, found the key operator there alone. His name was Kenny Reed, a youngster still in his teens, who had been trained to operate the key.

"Sheriff," Kenny said, "can I do anythin' for ya?"

"Kenny," Iron Horse said, "that telegram I sent last week."

"To your friend," Kenny said, "White Horse, wasn't it?"

"Yes, that one," Iron Horse said. "Did anyone else read it?"

"I don't show telegrams to anybody," Kenny said, defensively.

"But you keep copies, right?"

"Yessir."

"Could someone have broken in here and read them?" Iron Horse asked.

Kenny frowned and stroked his jaw.

"Kenny?"

"Somebody did break in here a coupla days later," the boy said. "I didn't think anythin' of it because nothin' was missin'."

"And the copies?"

"As far as I know they're all there."

"Would you check and see if mine is there, please?" Iron Horse asked.

"Sure thing, Sheriff."

Kenny went to a desk, opened the draw and took out a bunch of copies. He leafed through them once, and then again, before turning to Iron Horse.

"It's not here, Sheriff," he said. "Somebody stole it."

"That explains how they knew White Horse was coming," Iron Horse said, more to himself than to the flustered Kenny. "But who?"

"I dunno, Sheriff," Kenny said.

"You didn't see anybody hanging around this office, maybe waiting for it to close?"

"No sir."

A lot of people in town didn't like Iron Horse, so there were too many to consider.

"All right, Kenny," the lawman said, "thanks."

He left the telegraph office and stopped outside. He didn't know who else he could go to for help, and if he did, he probably wouldn't want to risk their lives. One dead friend was enough to deal with.

The only thing he could think of to do next was ride out to where White Horse's body had been found by a farmer who was coming into town for supplies and see what he could find in the area.

Chapter Three

Clint Adams had his face buried in Gloria Dennison's wet, fragrant pussy. The bushy hair between her legs was more golden and wispy than the hair on her lovely head.

They had only met the night before at a show in a local theater. Fort Worth, Texas was a growing metropolis, which meant new theaters and museums. The show Clint saw was a musical, and a bad one, but he noticed Gloria across the room. After the show, drinks were served in a lobby as the performers mingled with the audience. When Clint approached Gloria with two glasses of champagne, they proceeded to mingle only with each other. The mingling eventually made its way to his hotel room and his bed.

The first time they had sex was quick and intense. This time he was determined to taste and smell every inch of her. As he probed her with his tongue, she moaned, reached down and cupped his head in her hands.

"My God," she breathed, "you're so good at that."

"Only because you're so tasty," he told her. "And you smell wonderful."

"For Godssake, stop talking," she said, "and lick."

"Yes, Ma'am."

He directed his attention back to her pussy and by the time he took her over the edge, his face was soaked with her nectar. She drummed her heels on the mattress and wrapped her fingers in his hair until the waves of pleasure had passed, leaving her breathless . . .

***

"My bottom's too big," she said.

He reached over and rubbed it.

"Your bottom is just fine," he assured her.

"I'll bet most of the women you've been with were skinny," she said.

"Hardly," he said. "The fact is I don't like skinny women. I like my women to have some meat on their bones."

"Well," she said, "didn't you luck out with me."

"Don't forget," he said, "I saw you across the room and was drawn to you. Of course, your beautiful face had a lot to do with it, but so did your body."

"My big tits and bottom," she said.

"Among other things," he said.

"Well," she said, reaching out to stroke his cock, "I knew looking across the room that you'd be a beautiful man."

"I hardly think I qualify as beautiful," he said.

"I meant this," she said, gripping his penis.

"Oh."

She leaned over and pressed her cheek to his hot column of flesh.

"Mmmm, so smooth and hot," she said, licking him. "And tasty." She took his cock into her mouth, deeply, then in and out, slowly sucking it, getting it wet and slick with her saliva.

Clint closed his eyes and tried to relax and enjoy, but the more she sucked him the faster she went, and the more excited he got. Before long he was hard as a rock, and she still managed to take the length of him in. Instead of continuing to relax, he was trying not to explode into her mouth too soon. He gritted his teeth as he felt his load rushing up his legs. He always thought it started way down at his feet, worked its way up and then exploded out his cock. Sometimes he was able to fight it off, other times it just came up and shot out uncontrollably.

He was trying to control it this time, because from her moans and sighs he could tell she was enjoying herself. He didn't want it to end too soon for her. Finally, in the end, he figured they had the rest of the night, and he went off like a geyser . . .

***

Later, as they lay side-by-side, she asked, "When are you leaving town?"

"I was planning to leave tomorrow."

"To go where?"

"Nowhere in particular. And you?"

"I'm also leaving tomorrow."

"To go where?"

"Dallas."

"What's in Dallas?"

"More theater, I'm afraid. I was wondering if you'd come with me."

"I don't think so," he said. "I've had enough theater for a while."

"Yes," she agreed, "tonight was pretty bad."

"Why do you go to so much theater?"

"Oh, I didn't tell you," she said. "I review shows for a Texas newspaper."

"Ah."

"So I guess this will be our only night together," she said.

"That's true," he said.

"Well," she said, tossing a leg over him, "we might as well not waste it sleeping."

He turned toward her and said, "I was thinking the same thing."

Chapter Four

The next morning Clint and Gloria had breakfast, having worked up a hearty appetite together. He then saw her to her train and kissed her goodbye before going to the livery to collect his Tobiano.

He rode out of Fort Worth, heading south. As he had told Gloria, he was going nowhere in particular. But after three hours, things changed. He noticed a hitch in Toby's gait. He dismounted and checked the horse's legs, found the animal favoring one.

"What's wrong, Boy?" he asked, rubbing the leg.

The horse shook his head and shied away from Clint's touch.

"Sore, huh?" He stroked the horse's neck. "All right, we'll get you some help in the next town we come to."

He took the horse's reins and started walking with him.

***

The next town he and Toby came to was a place called Hellcat.

"What a lousy name for a town, huh, boy?" Clint asked Toby. "Hopefully there's someone there who can help us."

He continued toward the town, the horse limping along behind him. As they walked down the main street, Clint found it oddly quiet even for a small town.

"I don't know what's going on," Clint said, "but there's got to be a livery stable, or a vet."

He kept walking, still not seeing a soul, and finally spotted a stable ahead.

"Ah," he said to Toby, "here we go."

He walked the horse to the doors, tied off the reins and went inside.

"Hello?" he called. "Anyone here?"

It looked as if half the stalls were filled, the horses standing calmly.

"Hello?"

"Yeah, I'm here," a man said, coming from the back. "What can I do for ya?"

He was in his fifties, wearing a shapeless hat and an apron over denim trousers.

"Are you the hostler?" Clint asked.

"I am," the man said. "My name's Leo."

"Leo," Clint asked, "is there a vet in town?"

"That would be me, too," Leo said. "Hostler, blacksmith, vet."

"My horse seems to have come up lame, and I can't see why," Clint said. "You mind if I bring him in?"

"No, no," Leo said, "of course, bring him in. I'll take a look at him."

Clint went out to fetch Toby and walked the horse into the stable.

"Nice lookin' animal," Leo said. "A Tobiano, isn't he?"

"Yes."

Leo took the reins from Clint, walked Toby in a circle a few times.

"He's favoring the front left," Leo said. He leaned over and ran his hand gently over Toby's leg. At one point Toby whinnied and stepped back.

"That's it," Leo said. "Left fetlock joint. Did he take a bad step?"

"Not an obvious one," Clint said. "How bad?"

"It's pretty sore," Leo said. "I can take a closer look, but I don't think it's worse than that. You'll have to stay off him for a while."

"How long is a while?"

"I'll know more after I examine him fully," Leo said. "You're gonna be here at least overnight. You might as well get a hotel room and a meal."

"I'll do that," Clint said, stroking Toby's neck. "Tell me, what's going on in this town? Is it always this quiet?"

"It wasn't always quiet," Leo said. "This was a pretty wild town. For a long time we didn't have any law."

"Do you have any, now?"

"A sheriff," Leo said. "But there ain't many people in town who like 'im."

"Why not?"

"He's Apache."

"An Indian sheriff?"

Leo nodded.

"He's actually pretty good at it," the hostler said. "He's eastern educated. When he came back his own people didn't want him. Nobody wanted him here either, but when he realized we didn't have a sheriff, he volunteered for the job. That was six months ago."

"And things have changed?"

"A lot," Leo said. "But there are still those who don't want him here."

"What's that got to do with the streets being empty?"

"Well . . . seems the sheriff sent for a friend of his to be his deputy. Another Indian."

"And?"

"He was bushwhacked and killed before he could even get here," Leo said. "Just outside of town. That was

16

a few days ago. Since then, the sheriff's been lookin' for who did it. He's busted some heads while lookin'. Folks are afraid somebody's gonna try for him on the street, and nobody wants to get caught in the crossfire."

"I guess I can't blame them for that," Clint said. "How many hotels are in town?"

"Two," Leo said.

"Is one better than the other?"

"To tell the truth," Leo said, "one's as bad as the other. Don't try to eat in either dining room. There's a little café a few streets from here. That's where most people eat, so it's usually pretty crowded. But now that people are stayin' off the streets, not so much."

"Thanks, Leo," Clint said. "What do I owe you?"

"Nothin', yet."

He took his saddlebags and rifle off his horse and started for the door.

"Hey!" Leo said.

"Yeah"

"You didn't tell me your name."

"Adams," Clint said, "Clint Adams."

He didn't wait to see if the man recognized his name.

Chapter Five

Clint was eating a bowl of beef stew in the café a half an hour later. The waiter assured him it was the special. Clint didn't know how special it was, but it tasted all right.

There were a couple of other tables occupied, otherwise the place was empty.

When the man brought him some coffee Clint asked, "Expecting a supper rush?"

"Usually," the man said, "but not lately. Folks are expectin' trouble."

"For the sheriff?"

The waiter made a rude sound with his mouth.

"Sheriff," he said. "An Indian."

"Still," Clint said, "he *is* the law, right?"

"Only because no one else wanted the job," the waiter said.

"So somebody doesn't like him enough to kill him?" Clint asked.

"Not me," the waiter said, "but somebody, I guess."

"I heard his deputy was killed."

"Wasn't his deputy yet," the waiter said. "And he was just another savage."

"You don't like Indians?" Clint asked.

"Who does?"

The waiter left Clint his check and went back to the kitchen. Clint left the money on the table and walked to the door. The people at the other two tables—a couple, and a single man—ignored him.

He stepped out and checked both ways. No one was visible. He wondered how the local saloon would look. If his horse was going to need days to recover, he was going to need some way to spend his time. He could think of two: poker, or a woman.

He started walking, intending to stop in the first saloon he came to.

***

Leo, the hostler, entered the sheriff's office. Iron Horse looked up from his desk.

"Leo," he said.

"Somethin' I think you should know, Sheriff."

"What?"

"Clint Adams is in town."

Iron Horse didn't react.

"He's the Gunsmith."

"I know," the lawman said. "What's he doin' here?"

"His horse came up lame outside of town," Leo said. "But that don't mean he wasn't comin' here, anyway."

Again, Iron Horse didn't react.

"Somebody might've hired him to kill you," Leo commented.

After a moment Iron Horse said, "Thanks, Leo."

"Just thought you should know," the hostler said, and left.

Iron Horse stood and walked to the window. The street was still empty. Everyone was expecting a hailstorm of bullets any minute. Were they going to come from the Gunsmith's gun? Or was the man there just because his horse went lame? There was only one way to find out.

He left his office.

***

Clint found a saloon called The Nebraska Saloon. He was curious about the name. He went through the batwings, which squeaked.

He went to the bar and ordered a beer. The room was mid-size, with a few other patrons seated at tables. They all seemed to be waiting for something.

"What's with the name?" he asked the bartender.

"The owner's from Nebraska," the middle-aged man said. "I guess he's homesick." He went to the other end of the bar and wiped it with a rag.

Clint heard the squeak of the batwings and looked that way. He saw an Indian wearing a badge enter the saloon. The man looked at the bar, saw Clint and approached. He was in his early thirties, had long black hair with a bandana tied around his head, and was wearing a holstered Colt.

"Sheriff," Clint said, speaking first.

"Mr. Adams," the man said. "I heard you were in town. I'm Sheriff Iron Horse."

"I only just got here, and I've already heard about you, Sheriff," Clint said. "Can I buy you a drink?"

"That depends."

"On what?"

"On whether or not you're here to kill me."

Clint put his beer down on the bar and stared at the man for a few moments.

"What the hell—no, I'm not here to kill you. What would make you think that?"

"You've heard about my deputy?"

"Your almost-deputy, yeah," Clint said. "He was bushwhacked. I understand the town is expecting the same thing to happen to you."

"Unless somebody comes to town who's been hired to kill me," Iron Horse said.

"Well, if that does happen," Clint said, "it won't be me. I don't hire out my gun."

Iron Horse regarded Clint for a few moments, then said, "Okay, in that case, you can buy me a beer."

Chapter Six

Clint and Iron Horse took their beers to a table.

"If you're not here to kill me," Iron Horse said, "then I'm going to ask for your help."

"I'm stuck here at least overnight," Clint said, "maybe even longer, so go ahead and ask."

"It's fairly obvious somebody in town wants me dead," Iron Horse said. "My friend, White Horse, was coming to back me and be my deputy, but he was ambushed."

"Shot?"

Iron Horse nodded.

"In the back."

Backshooters got Clint's ire up.

"I hate that!" Clint said. "I hate cowards who can't act face-to-face."

"Then maybe you'll help me find them," Iron Horse said. "I'm not trained as a detective. In fact, I had no law enforcement experience when I took this job."

"Well," Clint said, "I've done some detective work with the Pinkertons, and with my friend, Talbot Roper, but I don't know anyone, or anything about this town."

"All I need you to do," Iron Horse said, "is keep me alive until I find the bushwhackers. Once I do that, I'm done with this job. These people haven't wanted me here all along, and I think I'm ready to grant them their wish."

"But not before you find out who killed your friend," Clint said.

"Right."

"I understand that."

"It's a lot to ask," Iron Horse said. "You don't even know me."

"Well," Clint said, "if you buy me another beer, I'll know you better."

"Done," Iron Horse said, and waved at the bartender.

The man brought over two more beers and took Iron Horse's money with obvious distaste.

"You see?" the Apache said. "It's obvious he doesn't want me here."

"But you're the law," Clint said. "How exactly did that happen? I heard nobody wanted the job, but how did you manage to get it?"

"I went to the mayor and volunteered to wear the badge," Iron Horse said. "The mayor was wary, but finally agreed to pin the badge on me, and pay me to keep the peace."

"Didn't he need to clear it with someone? A board of some kind?"

"No," Iron Horse said, "he just did it. People object-ed, but then I began to do the job, and the town became less of a hell hole."

"But the name."

Iron Horse nodded.

"Hellcat, yes. The mayor is determined to change it, but so far there's been resistance. Once I leave, though, I predict the town will revert to what it was before me. When that happens, they'll never change the name."

"I'm amazed, Sheriff, that you've been able to stay in a job, in a town, where the people don't want you."

"I have to admit," Iron Horse said, "that was part of the reason I wanted the job, to rub it in everyone's face that they needed to treat me like the law."

"But now you've had enough?"

Iron Horse sat back in his chair and shook his head.

"I should have left before I got White Horse killed," he said. "Now I won't leave until I have his killer or killers."

"If you can keep from being killed, yourself," Clint said.

"They bushwhacked him. I'm sure they'd bushwhack me, but if I had someone watching my back . . ."

Clint thought it over for a moment. He was stuck there, needed something to pass the time, and keeping the local lawman alive seemed a worthy undertaking.

Putting away a bushwhacker or bushwhackers in the process would be a cherry on top.

"I'll do it," Clint said.

"Good!" Iron Horse said. "I don't know how to thank you."

"Just don't make me wear a badge," Clint said.

Chapter Seven

Iron Horse told Clint the first thing he wanted to do was introduce him to the mayor.

"You mean you want to push me in his face," Clint said.

"Exactly."

"Let's do it," Clint said.

They left half their beers and headed for City Hall and the mayor's office.

It was a small building, and the mayor didn't have a secretary or an assistant. Iron Horse just knocked on the door of the man's office.

"Sheriff," Mayor Dandridge said. "What brings you here?"

"I want to introduce you to the man who's going to keep me alive until I find White Horse's killers."

The mayor looked surprised.

"A new deputy?"

"Not a deputy," Iron Horse said, "just a new friend. Mayor Dandridge, this is Clint Adams."

"Clint . . . Adams?" the mayor repeated. "You mean, the Gunsmith?"

"That's right."

"Well, uh, Sir," the mayor stammered. "It's good to, uh, meet you. What brings you to Hellcat?"

"A lame horse, mostly," Clint said. "While your hostler and vet is working on him, your sheriff asked for my help in staying alive." Clint shrugged. "It seemed like a worthy request to fill."

"Well," Dandridge said to Iron Horse, "lucky for you."

"And unlucky for whoever the bushwhackers are," Iron Horse said. "Now that I don't have to worry about being bushwhacked myself, I'll find them."

"I hope so, Sheriff," the mayor said. "I hope so." He seemed to have regained his composure. "Mr. Adams, we're grateful for your help."

"My pleasure, Mr. Mayor," Clint said. "If I can keep the sheriff from being shot in the back, I'm glad to do it." He glared at the man. "I hate backshooters!"

"I, uh, I don't blame you," the mayor said.

"We'll leave you to your work," Iron Horse said, "and we'll get to mine."

"Uh, keep me, uh, informed," the mayor said, seemingly unnerved by Clint's look.

Iron Horse and Clint left the office, and the building.

"You think he had anything to do with White Horse's death?" Clint asked.

"I didn't," Iron Horse said, "but you seemed to make him nervous."

"Yeah, I did, didn't I."

"What's behind your hatred of backshooters? It seems . . . intense. Were you ever shot in the back?"

"I was, once," Clint said, "but I've hated them ever since my friend, Bill Hickok, was killed by one."

That surprised Iron Horse.

"You knew Wild Bill Hickok?"

"I knew him well," Clint said. "I lost a good friend when Jack McCall shot him in Deadwood."

"Well," Iron Horse started, "I lost a good friend when Charlie White Horse was killed by one, so we have that in common. Let's go to my office and I'll tell you what I have so far."

***

After Sheriff Iron Horse and Clint Adams left his office Mayor Dandridge went to his window and watched the two men walk away. The Apache had done a good job for six months, but it was time for him to give up the badge. At least, that was what the mayor was thinking before Clint Adams entered the picture. With the Gunsmith at his side, Iron Horse was going to be hard to get rid of.

Dandridge left the building and headed for the telegraph office.

***

In the sheriff's office Iron Horse poured two mugs of coffee and handed Clint one.

"Sorry, it's strong."

"Just the way I like it," Clint said.

Both men sat. Iron Horse opened his desk drawer and put two things on the desktop.

"I've got this, and this," he said, pointing.

Clint picked up the bullet.

"Forty-four forty," he said. "Winchester. This the bullet that killed your friend?"

Iron Horse nodded.

"The undertaker dug it out for me," he said. "This and the other one I found out near where White Horse was killed."

"This" was the spent cartridge.

"How far away was it?" Clint asked.

"About twenty feet."

Clint put the bullet down.

"So with this bullet, and that distance, it could have been a rifle or a handgun."

"Right," Iron Horse said. "I'm just surprised someone was able to get that close to White Horse without him noticing. We're looking for someone who was able to sneak up on an Apache."

"Another Apache?" Clint asked.

"I doubt it," Iron Horse said, "but probably somebody who moves like an Apache."

"I'd think that's somebody you could find, Sheriff," Clint said.

"And I will," Iron Horse said, "as long as I'm alive to do it. That's where you come in."

Clint raised his coffee mug and said, "I'll do my best."

Chapter Eight

"I'm going to start by showing you a good place to eat supper," Iron Horse said. "I go there because nobody else does."

"How do they stay in business?" Clint asked.

"I ask them the same question," Iron Horse said. "Come on."

Iron Horse led Clint from the office along several streets, and then down a side street to a small storefront that looked as if it had been boarded up.

"There's a business here?" Clint asked.

"I guess you could call it that," Iron Horse said.

The Apache opened the front door and waved at Clint to precede him. Once inside Clint saw a large, clean room with tables and chairs.

"Looks like they spent most of their money fixing the inside up," Clint said. "The outside's not likely to attract many people."

"I do not want many people," a voice said, as a man stepped into the room. He was an older Indian, beefy and built low to the ground. He was a powerful looking man who seemed off wearing an apron.

"Sheriff," he said.

"Big Man," Iron Horse said. "This is Clint Adams. He is going to help me find out who killed White Horse."

"Very good," Big Man said.

Clint thought the name odd, as the man was stocky and short, not very tall. Although the Big Man name could have referred to anything.

"Would you gents like somethin' to eat?"

"That is why we are here," Iron Horse said.

"Sit anywhere and I'll bring it."

Iron Horse and Clint sat at a table against one wall.

"He didn't ask us what we want," Clint said.

"When you come here, you eat what Big Man cooks," Iron Horse explained. "There is no menu."

"I see," Clint said.

"The Whites in town don't come here, which suits Big Man fine."

"And you and Big Man, you're old friends?"

"No," Iron Horse said, "we met here in town."

"Is he Apache?"

"Sioux," Iron Horse said. "But we get along."

"Does he get along with anyone else in town?"

"Very few," Iron Horse said.

Big Man came out with two cups of coffee and set them down, then returned to the kitchen.

"Strong and black," Iron Horse said. "He doesn't drink coffee, but he knows how to make it."

Clint sipped and said, "He sure does."

When Big Man returned, he was carrying two plates of steaming food. As he set them down, Clint saw that it looked like some sort of chicken, surrounded by an array of vegetables.

"Enjoy," Big Man said.

As the man went back to the kitchen, Clint said to Iron Horse, "Chicken?"

"Wild pheasant. He goes out hunting them himself."

"Does he have any help here?" Clint asked. "Not that he needs any."

"He has one person helping him," Iron Horse said. "His daughter."

"A little girl?"

"Not so little," Iron Horse said. "She is twenty, and beautiful."

"She's here now?"

"She's in the kitchen, I'm sure," Iron Horse said. "Big Man is very protective of her."

"Do I get to meet her?"

"Maybe," Iron Horse said. "That's up to Big Man."

They set about eating and discussing how to proceed.

"You must know who in town hates Apaches," Clint said.

"Yes, I do," Iron Horse said. "Almost everyone."

"Anyone with enough money to hire it done?"

"That would narrow it down some," Iron Horse said. "There are a couple of ranchers who used to let their hands ride into town and raise hell. They would shoot the town up, and assault some of the saloon girls."

"And you stopped all that?"

"Yes, I had to break a few heads to do it, but they finally stopped coming."

"Is there another town nearby that they switched to?"

"A few," Iron Horse said. "But I haven't checked to see which one. I was only concerned with getting them to stop coming here."

"Which I'm sure the saloon owners didn't like," Clint said.

"Right," Iron Horse said. "We have two saloons. Each of the owners would have the money to hire a killer."

"Who are they?"

"The Nebraska is owned by John Nettles. The other one, The Lady Gay, is owned by Daisy DuValier."

"Let me guess," Clint said. "A tough lady."

"Pretty tough," Iron Horse said. "The first time I chased the men from her place she took a swing at me."

"And Nettles?"

"He didn't take a swing," Iron Horse said, "but he wanted to."

"Then I guess we should start with them, shouldn't we?" Clint said. "That is, after we have some more of the tasty pheasant."

Chapter Nine

Clint and Iron Horse walked to The Nebraska. A lot seemed to have happened since Clint first met the sheriff there, only hours before. Suddenly, he was embroiled in the sheriff's relationship with the town, and his search for his friend, White Horse's, killer.

They came through the batwings together, attracting attention from the men drinking and gambling as they approached the bar.

"Is Mr. Nettles here?" Iron Horse asked.

"He's in his office," the barkeep said.

"Should we just go back," Clint asked, "or would you prefer to announce us?"

"Announce you," the bartender repeated, looking amused. "Yeah, sure I'll announce you. Sheriff Iron Horse and . . .?"

"Clint Adams," Clint said.

The man looked stunned, then said, "Oh, Mr. Adams. I, uh, I didn't know you was here. You can go back."

"No," Clint said, "I think you should announce us."

"Oh, oh, okay."

The barman came around from behind the bar and went to the back of the room.

"Announce us?" Iron Horse asked. "Are we royalty?"

"I just wanted to make him walk back there," Clint said.

The man went through a doorway, then came out and returned to the bar.

"Mr. Nettles will see you now, Mr. Adams, Sheriff."

"Thanks," Clint said.

He and Iron Horse walked to the back and knocked on the door.

"Come!"

They entered, and the tall, handsome man behind the desk stood up.

"Sheriff," he said, "Mr. Adams, to what do I owe this pleasure?"

"I wanted to talk to you about the shooting of my deputy, Charlie White Horse."

Nettles frowned.

"I understood he was shot before you could deputize him."

"As far as I'm concerned, he was my deputy as soon as he agreed to come here."

"And now your deputy is the Gunsmith?"

"No," Clint answered, "I'm in town because my horse went lame. But I've agreed to keep the sheriff alive while he finds his killer or killers."

Nettles looked at Iron Horse and sat back down behind his desk.

"Why come to me?"

"Because when I put on this badge," Iron Horse said, "I cut into your business."

"Yeah," Nettles said, "you did do that. What makes you think I'd kill your deputy for that reason?"

"Somebody hired a professional to get it done," Iron Horse said. "You have money."

"Why would I hire someone to kill a man I don't even know?" the saloon owner asked.

"To make it easier to get to me," Iron Horse said.

"You're going down the wrong trail, Sheriff," Nettles said. "I have better things to do with my money. And believe me, despite your efforts to harm my business, I have plenty of it."

"So you are saying you had nothing to do with my deputy's death," Iron Horse said. "And you have no intention of coming after me."

"That's exactly what I'm saying," Nettles replied. "You'll have to look somewhere else. Try across the street? Miss Daisy sure has enough money to hire it done."

"That is my next stop," Iron Horse said.

"Let me know how it turns out."

Nettles turned his attention to some papers on his desk.

Clint stepped forward and slapped his hand down on the paper. Nettles jumped back in his chair, slamming into the wall.

"If we find out you did have anything to do with White Horse's death," Clint said, "we'll be back."

He turned and walked to the door, followed by Sheriff Iron Horse.

***

After Clint and Iron Horse left the office, another door to the right of the desk opened and Mayor Dandridge stepped out.

"I told you the Gunsmith was here," he said to Nettles.

"Yes, you did," Nettles said, "and if you hadn't pinned that badge on the Apache six months ago, we wouldn't be in this mess."

"Granted," the mayor said, "but now what do we do?"

"We sit back," Nettles said, "and wait."

"Just wait?"

"You sent your telegram, didn't you?" Nettles asked.

"I did, before I came here."

"Then yes, Mr. Mayor," Nettles said, "we just sit here and wait."

Chapter Ten

Clint and Iron Horse went directly to the saloon doors and out. They stopped just outside.

"What do you think?" Iron Horse asked.

"He's slippery," Clint said.

"Yes, he is. But is he our man?"

"Well, he's certainly trying to put us on another trail," Clint commented.

"Daisy DuValier."

"What do you know about her, other than she owns a saloon."

"I heard she came here from New Orleans."

Clint looked surprised.

"Why would anyone do that?" he wondered. "From New Orleans to Hellcat, Texas?"

"I can't answer that."

"Well, I may be able to," Clint said. "I'll just have to send a telegram. But I'd like to meet the lady, first."

"Ready for another beer, then?" Iron Horse asked.

"Always," Clint said.

They stepped into the street and crossed over to the Lady Gay Saloon.

As they entered, Clint saw the difference in a saloon run by a woman rather than a man. The Gay was brighter, cleaner, had more girls working the floor, though they were classy looking rather than scantily clad. In one corner a piano player was tinkling the ivories, though not harshly or loudly.

The only similarity to the Nebraska was that, as they approached the bar, eyes followed them.

"Sheriff," the bartender said, with a smile. "Help ya?"

"We'd like to see Miss Daisy," Iron Horse said.

"Sure thing," the barman said. "I'm sure she'd like to see you. Follow me."

Rather than lead the men to a door in the back of the room, he took them to the stairs to the second level. There they walked down a hall to a door, which the man knocked on.

"Come in," a woman's voice called.

He opened the door.

"Miss Daisy, the sheriff and a friend of his are here to see you."

"Send them in, Al."

The bartender looked at them and said, "You can go in."

"Thank you," Iron Horse said. He led Clint into the room.

"Sheriff Iron Horse," a well-dressed, equally well turned-out woman greeted. She was dark-haired, in her forties, and lovely. She stood with a mirrored dressing table behind her. "To what do I owe this visit?"

"Miss DuValier," Iron Horse said, "this is Clint Adams."

"Well," she said, eyeing Clint up and down, "I'm even more curious to know why the Gunsmith is in my place."

"He's in town to help me," Iron Horse said.

"Is this about your friend who was killed?"

"My deputy, yes," Iron Horse said.

"I didn't think you had time to deputize him," she said.

He told her the same thing he'd told John Nettles.

"That made her look at Clint, and he headed her off.

"I'm not a deputy," he said, "I'm just here to help."

"Help find the killer?"

"Help keep the sheriff alive so he can find the killer," Clint corrected.

She looked at Iron Horse.

"You expect to be bushwhacked?"

"Every day," Iron Horse said.

"Then I'm glad you have help," she said. "What can I do for you, Sheriff?"

"I'm going to ask you the same questions I asked Mr. Nettles, across the street."

"Ah . . ." she said. "You want to know if I had anything to do with the killing."

"Did you?"

"No, Sheriff, I did not," she said. "I didn't shoot your friend, and I didn't hire anyone to have it done."

"And would you be heartbroken if the same thing happened to the sheriff?" Clint asked.

"Heartbroken? No," she admitted, "but I wouldn't be happy about it."

"But he'd be gone from office, and you'd probably get a large part of your customers back again."

"Yes, the rowdy part," she said. "I don't mind not having that faction in my place. And the same thing could be accomplished if the sheriff just stepped down. So no, I don't want him dead." She looked at Iron Horse. "Anything else?"

"That would be about it," Iron Horse answered.

"What's your next move?" she asked.

"There are other people who have enough money to hire a killer," Iron Horse said. "We are going to talk to them all."

"Well, I wish you luck with the ranchers," she said. "They're even more upset with you than anyone as far as barring their hands from town."

"Barring those with guns," Iron Horse corrected. "It is their choice not to come to town without guns. Thank you for seeing us, Miss DuValier."

"Come back for a drink later," she said, looking at Clint. "First one will be on the house."

"I might just do that," Clint said.

He and Iron Horse left the room, went down the stairs and out to the street.

"Did you find her as slippery as Nettles was?" Iron Horse asked.

"In a much smoother way," Clint said, "but yes."

"Wait until you meet the ranchers."

"Do we have time today?"

"We'll head out in the morning," Iron Horse said. "We can see them all in one day."

"So what now?" Clint asked.

"I have my rounds to make."

"I'll make them with you," Clint said. "Start my assignment to keep you alive."

"You could go get some rest," the sheriff said. "You only rode in today."

"That's true, but making your rounds with you is the best way for me to watch your back, Sheriff," Clint pointed out to the man.

"Good point," Iron Horse said.

Chapter Eleven

Clint made rounds with the lawman, then accompanied him to his office and stayed with him until darkness fell.

"I'm going to turn in so we can get an early start in the morning," Iron Horse said.

"I'll walk with you until you get home," Clint said.

The sheriff had been given a small house at the south end of town. When they reached it, Iron Horse turned to Clint.

"It occurs to me that word will have got out now about you being here," he said. "While you're watching my back, who is going to be watching yours?"

"I've been watching my own back for a lot of years, Sheriff," Clint said. "But do you really think someone would try to bushwhack one of us in town?"

"You are right," Iron Horse said. "It will probably happen while we're riding out to see the ranchers."

"We'll be doubly alert tomorrow then. Good night."

"Good night, Mr. Adams."

"Just call me Clint."

"My first name is Samuel," Iron Horse said, "but I prefer Sheriff or Iron Horse."

"Good night, Sheriff."

***

Clint's first thought was to go to his hotel, but he decided to stop by the Lady Gay, again. He had the feeling Daisy DuValier had invited him back for a reason. Perhaps she had something she wanted to tell him.

"Back again?" Al, the bartender asked, as he presented himself at the bar.

"Miss Daisy promised me the first one on the house," Clint said.

"She mentioned it," the bartender said. "Comin' up."

As he set the beer in front of him Clint asked, "Is the lady around?"

"She'll be down soon," Al said. "It's gettin' busy."

Clint looked and saw that Al was right. Most of the tables were now occupied, gaming was going on, the piano was still going, and the girls were busy on the floor.

"Must've been busier than this before Sheriff Iron Horse came along," he said.

"This busy, but rowdier," the bartender said. "Fights, and gunplay."

"Anyone killed?"

"Just lots of property damage."

"Miss Daisy didn't mind?"

"Not so long as the property damage was paid for," Al said.

"So she wasn't happy when the sheriff kept the ranch hands out of town."

"I think she understands it was their choice not to come to town without their guns," Al said.

"So she'd have no reason to hire anybody to kill the sheriff, or his deputy."

"Naw," Al said. "That wouldn't be Miss Daisy's style. Now Nettles, across the street, he'd do somethin' like that."

"He would?"

"Oh yeah," Al said. "That is, he's got men who'd do it for him."

"Like who?"

"Al?"

They both turned to look at Daisy DuValier, standing at the bar a few feet from him. "You talk too much."

"That's true," Al said. "Champagne, boss?"

"Yes," She said, "bring it and whatever Mr. Adams is drinking to my table. Mr. Adams?"

"Yes, Ma—" Clint started, but she turned and walked away, so he followed her. She led him to a table in the back of the room, greeting customers along the way.

They sat across from each other, and the bartender set down their drinks.

"Miss DuValier," Clint said.

"Call me Daisy, and I'll call you Clint."

"Okay, Daisy. Why did I get the feeling you were inviting me back here to tell me something?"

"Well, first, you're the Gunsmith," she said. "I don't want to be on the wrong side of you. And second, you're almost the law."

"I'm not—"

"Yes, I know," she said. "You're not a deputy. But you're close enough."

"So?"

"So your friend, the sheriff, is on the wrong trail if he's looking at me," she said.

"Whose trail should he be on?"

"Well, I can't tell you who he should be after, just who he shouldn't be after."

"You."

"Right."

"And you want to convince me of that."

"Yes," she said. "How do I do that?"

Clint hesitated, then said, "Give me a minute and I'll think of a way."

Chapter Twelve

"Why would someone leave New Orleans to come to a place like Hellcat, Texas?" Clint asked.

"Is this how I can convince you?" she asked. "Answer questions?"

"It's a good way to start."

"I can think of better ways," she said, wetting her lips with champagne.

"Let's get to that later," Clint said. "I'm going to send a telegram to someone I know in New Orleans, so you might as well tell me the truth."

She studied him for a moment, then said, "You won't find out anything about me in New Orleans."

"Why? Did you come here from somewhere else?"

"No," she said, "but in New Orleans by name wasn't Daisy DuValier."

"What was your name?"

"I can't tell you that," she said. "I crossed paths with the wrong people and had to leave. I became Daisy and picked out this little town."

"Why not go somewhere further away from New Orleans?" Clint asked. "Like up north?"

"I don't like cold weather," she said. "I'm a hopeless Southerner."

"There are still other places you could go."

"And yet, I chose here."

"So what's your real name?"

She leaned back and played with her champagne glass, twirling it.

"I can't tell you that, Clint," she said. "Not yet, anyway. Maybe when I get to know you better."

He nodded and sipped his beer.

"You're still going to send that telegram, aren't you?" she asked.

"Yes," he said. "I know people who might find out something."

"Well," she said, "let me know what you find so I can confirm or deny it."

"Deal," he said. "Meanwhile, you must have some ideas about who did it, if you didn't."

"Nettles?" she said. "One of the rich ranchers?"

"We're going to talk to some of the ranchers tomorrow."

"That should be fun," she said. "They all hate Iron Horse."

"What about you?" he asked. "Do you hate Indians?"

"I've had nothing to do with Indians," she said. "All I know is what I've read or heard. I don't hold any of that against one man."

"You seem to be a very logical woman."

"I am," she said. "If you find out anything you'll see that it was logical for me to leave New Orleans and come here."

"I'll let you know," he said. "Anything else to tell me?"

"Not at the moment," she said, "but come back when you have some free time."

He finished his beer and said, "I'll do that."

***

After a quick, unsatisfactory breakfast in his hotel— he wouldn't eat there again—Clint went to Iron Horse's office after borrowing a horse from Leo at the livery.

"Yours'll be okay after a few days' rest," Leo told him. "But this one'll do the job for you, meantime."

It was a sturdy, six-year-old sorrel. He walked the horse to the telegraph office and sent one telegram to New Orleans. Then tied the horse off next to a roan he figured was the sheriff's and entered the man's office.

"Good morning," Iron Horse said. "Ready to go?"

"All set," Clint said. "Did you eat breakfast?"

"At home," Iron Hose said. "You?"

"In my hotel," Clint said. "I won't do that again."

"You're welcome at Big Man's any time," Iron Horse said. "Or the café would do."

"I'll make sure I eat at one of them," Clint said.

Iron Horse rose and came around from behind his desk.

"I figure we'll start with the ranch furthest from town, and then work our way closer."

"You're the boss," Clint said.

They stepped outside and mounted their horses.

"Looks like Leo did all right by you with that one," Iron Horse said.

"He's a sturdy enough horse," Clint said.

As they rode out of town, Clint told Iron Horse about talking with Daisy the night before.

"Do you think she was just trying to convince you she was innocent?" the Apache asked.

"If she was, she did a good job."

"So you're crossing her off our list?"

"Let's say I'm dropping her to the bottom," Clint replied, then added, "for now."

Chapter Thirteen

They spent the day talking to different ranchers, re-
ceiving a variety of reactions. One man ordered them off
his property before finally agreeing to answer a few
questions. Others responded unwillingly and unkindly,
but answered questions, nevertheless. Each time they
rode up to the main house they received unhappy or
hostile looks from ranch hands. By the end of the day,
with dusk falling, they were approaching town after
having talked with half a dozen ranchers.

"For a town this small I'm surprised there are so
many big spreads in the area," Clint commented.

"There are other towns," Iron Horse said. "One of the
reasons the mayor wants to change the town name is that
he thinks it will grow faster."

"Without the word 'hell' in the name?"

"Probably what he thinks," Iron Horse said.

"What do you think?"

"I think the town will grow when it has a different
mayor, and some reasonable business owners. It also has
to get rid of people like John Nettles."

"And Daisy DuValier?"

"I would've said yes, before you spoke with her last night," Iron Horse said. "I'm willing to give her the benefit of the doubt, since she seems willing to do the same with me."

Clint had an itch between his shoulders. Before the shot, he launched himself from his horse, hit Iron Horse around the waist and took both of them to the ground. There was a second shot as they rolled and took cover in a ditch by the side of the road.

When they stopped rolling Clint asked, "Are you hit?"

"No, you?"

"No."

They both peered up, Iron Horse with his gun in his hand. Clint's gun was in his holster, since there was nothing for him to shoot at.

"See anything?" Clint asked.

"No," Iron Horse said, "and I didn't feel anything, but you did."

"Just an itch."

"An itch I used to have," Iron Horse said. "I've become too domesticated." Iron Horse seemed very annoyed with himself. "I'm an Apache, damn it."

"You didn't feel anything, and apparently neither did your friend, White Horse. Whoever this is, he has to be good."

Iron Horse sank down into the ditch and leaned back.

"Well, thank the spirits you felt it. I guess I was right to ask you for help."

Clint sank down next to the Apache.

"Whoever it was, I think they're gone. Probably just as upset with themselves that they missed."

"They didn't bank on you being so good," Iron Horse said. "Hey, before we get our horses, I have a question."

"What is it?"

"Why?"

"Why what?"

"Why did you agree to help me? You don't know me."

"And I didn't know White Horse," Clint said, "but I don't like that he was bushwhacked."

"So there's no other reason but that you hate back-shooters?"

"I think that's a pretty good one, don't you?" Clint asked. "Also, I couldn't just stand by and watch a lawman get shot down."

"But you'll be on your way, soon."

"I'm here for a few days, at least," Clint said. "I'd still have to stand by and watch. I couldn't do that."

"Well, I'm already grateful," Iron Horse said. "Let's run down our horses and get back to town before our shooter repositions himself."

"I think he lit out when he missed," Clint said.

Their horses had not gone far and they were able to round them up fairly easily.

"Where do you think he fired from?" Iron Horse asked.

Clint pointed and said, "Up there, seems likely."

"Let's see if he left anything behind," Iron Horse said.

They rode up a rise where they thought the shots may have come from. While Clint kept watch, Iron Horse dismounted and walked the area, studying the ground. Finally, he saw the dying light glint off something, and picked it up. He walked back to Clint and held out his hand. Sitting in his palm was a 44.40 shell, like the one left by White Horse's killer.

"Same gun," Clint said.

"It sounded like a rifle," Iron Horse said, putting the shell in his shirt pocket.

"I agree," Clint said.

Iron Horse mounted up.

"Well, he made his try for one of us," the Apache said. "You or me?"

"Hard to know," Clint said. "But I'm sure he's not finished."

"Agreed," Iron Horse said. "Let's see if next time he tries in town, where he can get closer."

"If he does that," Clint said, "he better not miss."

Chapter Fourteen

Clint and Iron Horse left their mounts at the livery and went to Big Man's for supper. There was one other table with two men at it. Both of them looked like Apaches to Clint.

"Shawnee," Iron Horse said. "They would have snuck into town a back way to get here."

Clint was about to say something when a girl came out of the kitchen carrying plates to the Shawnee's table. She was an absolutely beautiful Indian girl, no doubt Big Man's daughter. Her long black hair shimmered, and her long apron did nothing to hide the curves of her firm young body.

"I told you," Iron Horse said. "Beautiful."

"She is that," Clint said, watching the girl walk back to the kitchen. Big Man came out and walked to their table.

"The food's comin'," he said. "Coffee?"

"Yes," Iron Horse said.

"Definitely."

"Comin' up."

Clint was hoping the girl would bring it, but she was probably cooking, because Big Man appeared with two mugs.

"What's the girl's name?" Clint asked, over the coffee.

"Little Deer," Iron Horse said. "She wants to be called Lisa, but her father won't have it."

"I assume she has the attention of the young men in town," Clint said.

"Big Man keeps her inside," Iron Horse said. "He'd kill any man who touched her. I'd keep that in mind, if I was you."

"She's beautiful," Clint said, "but young."

Big Man returned with plates that were piled with beef and vegetables. Little Deer followed behind with a basket of biscuits.

"Hello, Sheriff," she greeted.

"Little Deer," Iron Horse said, "this is Clint Adams."

"Hello, Mr. Adams."

"Back to the kitchen!" Big Man growled.

"Yes, Papa."

Big Man looked at Clint and said, "She is very young."

"I can see that," Clint said.

"Good," Big Man said. "Remember it!"

As the man returned to the kitchen, Clint looked at Iron Horse and asked, "What did I do?"

"It's not what you did," Iron Horse said, "it is how you looked at her."

"Jesus," Clint said, "she's a pretty girl, who wouldn't look at her?"

"Just be careful," Iron Horse said.

"I'm just going to pay attention to my food," Clint said.

"Good idea."

They both did that and discussed their day.

"Talking to the ranchers didn't help us much," Clint said. "They all had pretty much the same attitude, though some were more aggressive than others."

"And they all had time to send that bushwhacker after us," Iron Horse said.

"Maybe we should check at the mercantile," Clint said.

"What for?"

"Somebody may have bought some forty-four forties, recently."

"That's a good idea," Iron Horse said. "It wouldn't necessarily be the shooter, but it would give us a way to go."

"And I want to check and see if my telegram brought a reply," Clint said. "I asked the key operator to leave it at my hotel."

"After that we can make my rounds," Iron Horse said.

"Yes," Clint said, carefully. "Missing us today might push the shooter into something reckless."

***

After supper they left Big Man's and went to Clint's hotel. The desk clerk handed him a telegram that he said had come a short time ago.

"Thanks."

"Sure thing, Mr. Adams," the clerk said, nervously. Having the Gunsmith in the hotel—not to mention the sheriff's presence—was making him jumpy.

Outside the hotel Clint unfolded it and read.

"Anything?" Iron Horse said.

"I have a friend in New Orleans who thinks Daisy sounds like a woman named Yvette Cormier," Clint said. "If this is right, then Daisy was telling the truth when she said she crossed some bad people."

"Hopefully, sending your telegram didn't alert anyone that she is here," Iron Horse said.

"My friend's discreet," Clint said. But as he folded the telegram and put it in his pocket, he was thinking the same thing. If Daisy wasn't behind the bushwhacker, he would hate to cause her any trouble.

"Maybe you should warn her," Iron Horse said. "If she is this Yvette Cormier, she should know that you found out."

"I will," Clint said, "after we do your rounds."

Chapter Fifteen

The sheriff's rounds went quietly, with no sign of a bushwhacker in town. But the streets were still pretty deserted.

"People are still expecting trouble," Clint said.

"That makes all of us," Iron Horse said.

"Do you ever wish you had stayed back East?" Clint asked.

"No," Iron Horse said, without hesitation. "I was even less welcome there."

"What will you do after this job?" Clint asked.

"I might go into hibernation, somewhere," Iron Horse said. "Maybe the mountains. It's pretty obvious I am not welcome anywhere."

"I feel that way sometimes, too," Clint said.

"You? Why?"

"I live by my gun," Clint said. "That's a way of living that seems to be fading."

"Why not give it up, then?" Iron Horse asked.

"It's too late for that," Clint explained. "The first time I appear in public with no gun, I'm a dead man."

"I suppose that's true," Iron Horse said. "Have you ever considered the mountains?"

Clint laughed.

"I've been to the mountains," he said. "That life's not for me. Too many bears and wildcats."

"I might like bears and wildcats more than I like people," Iron Horse said. "Do you want to go and see Daisy? I can come with you and have a beer. It'll give people something to glare at."

"Sure, let's go."

Finished with rounds and sure that all doors supposed to be locked were, they headed for The Lady Gay.

***

When they entered, they saw the place was half full. Clint wondered how all these people had gotten there when they were staying off the street?

"If you're lookin' for Miss Daisy, she should be down shortly," Al, the bartender, said.

"Two beers while we wait, Al," Clint said.

"Gotcha."

The bartender set two beers in front of them. Iron Horse turned around so everyone in the room could see the Apache drinking firewater.

"You're pushing it," Clint said.

"You're probably right," Iron Horse said, "but I can't help it. Many of these people owe their quiet life to me.

Others hold it against me. And almost all of them want me out of my job. That's probably the main reason I stay in it." Iron Horse looked at Clint. "Why did you say you'd help me if I didn't make you wear a badge?"

"I did my time behind a badge early in my life," Clint said. "In fact, I was Jim Hickok's deputy for a while. But I've been a deputy, as well as a sheriff and a marshal. I always found that people resented me and were never willing to help. Wherever I worked, they felt if anything went wrong it was my responsibility alone. I don't like when people don't lift a finger to help themselves because they have a lawman."

"I guess you're right," Iron Horse said. "I don't think I'll ever wear a badge again after this."

They turned back to the bar just as Daisy DuValier made her appearance. She stopped at the top of the stairs, either to take a look around, or to give everyone a chance to look at her. She wore a flowing yellow gown, with her shoulders and top slopes of her breasts showing. Most of the men in the room caught their breath at the sight of her, including Clint.

"Wow," Iron Horse said, "quite a sight."

She came down the stairs, walked across the room to join them at the bar. Men moved aside for her.

"Champagne?" Al asked.

"Of course," she said, "and fresh beers for my friends, here."

Iron Horse held up his hand.

"One's enough for me," he said.

"I'll take another before I make sure the sheriff gets home safe and sound."

"All right," Iron Horse said, "if you're going to make me wait, I'll have another."

Three men entered the saloon at that point, raucously. They were hollering as if already drunk. They were wearing trail clothes, and each had a holstered gun. They went to the far end of the bar and one of them slapped his hand down on it.

"Whisky, bartender!" he snapped.

"Go ahead, Al," Daisy said.

As the bartender moved down to that end of the bar Daisy asked Clint, "Well? Did you send your telegram?"

"I did," Clint said, "And I got a reply."

"And?"

"It's something we should talk about in private," Clint said.

"That'll be my pleasure," she said. "I'm going to go and socialize. After you've walked the sheriff home, come back and we'll talk. Good night, Sheriff."

"Good night, Miss Daisy."

She moved away with her champagne glass in hand.

"I thought Indians wasn't supposed to drink?" one of the noisy men shouted.

Chapter Sixteen

"Hey, look!" another man shouted. "He's wearin' a badge. I guess that makes a difference."

"You mean savages wearin' a badge don't get drunk?" the first man asked.

The three men looked around, swinging their whiskey glasses so that some of the liquid spilled.

"What kinda town is this that's got a savage as a lawman?" the first man asked.

Clint could feel Iron Horse stiffen.

"Easy," he said. "They're just drunk."

"They're drunks with big mouths and guns," Iron Horse said. "That is just the kind of thing I outlawed in this town." He put his beer down. "You can stay here. I can handle this."

Clint watched from where he was as Iron Horse approached the three men but stayed ready.

"You gents need to quiet it down," Iron Horse said.

"Whataya say, boy?" the first man asked. "Sheriff Savage says we need to be quiet."

"And I'll take your guns," Iron Horse went on.

"What?"

"No drunks with guns in this town," Iron Horse said. "It's the law."

"Whose law?" the first man asked.

"The town law," Iron Horse said, "and since I'm the sheriff, my law."

"Is this for real?" one of the other men asked loudly. He squinted at Iron Horse. "What're you, a Comanche?"

"I'm Apache," Iron Horse said.

"Apache?" The man's eyes went wide. "An Apache lawman?"

The three men laughed.

"I tell you what, Apache lawman," the first man said, "you back off and we'll let you walk out of here."

It occurred to Clint that this might be the follow-up to the attempted bushwhacking earlier in the day. Somebody could have sent these three in to brace Iron Horse.

"I do not want to tell the three of you again," Iron Horse said. "Put your guns on the bar."

"Or what?" the first man asked.

"Or you are going to jail for the night," Iron Horse said.

The three men stepped away from the bar, and suddenly didn't seem so drunk. Clint took a couple of steps and stood ready.

The other customers left their tables and places at the bar, moving to one side of the room.

"You're gonna hafta take our guns, Sheriff," the first man said.

"And if you take a step toward us, we'll kill ya," one of the others said.

"Whoa, boys!" Daisy DuValier's voice rang out. She stepped from a crowd of men who had gathered around her to protect her. "This is my place. No gunplay, here."

"Stand aside, lady," the first man said. "This'll be over in a minute."

"I told you—"

"I said stand aside!" the man shouted at her.

A couple of her customers stepped forward to grab Daisy and pull her back.

"Now the rest is up to you, Sheriff," the man said. "Looks like you're here all alone, so make your play."

"Not quite alone," Clint said, stepping forward and standing next to Iron Horse.

"And who's this?" one man asked. "The savage's deputy?"

"I'm not a lawman," Clint said. "Just a concerned citizen."

"Backin' the savage's play?"

"Well," Clint said, "actually, I'm offended by the way you spoke to the lady."

"Hey," the third man spoke for the first time, "he's a gentleman."

"Well, look, gentleman," the first man said, "we'll take care of you after the sheriff."

"No," Clint said, "I think I want to be taken care of now."

"The business of the law comes first, Clint," Iron Horse said.

"Clint?" the second man said.

"This is my friend, Clint Adams," Iron Horse said.

"Clint . . . Adams?" the third man said. "The Gunsmith.?

"Look, friend," Iron Horse said, "put your guns on the bar and we'll forget all about this."

"Bill . . ." the second man said to the first.

"Not a chance," Bill said. "We came here to do . . ."

". . . a job?" Iron Horse asked. "Somebody hired you to come here?"

"I didn't say that," the middle man, Bill, said.

"You fellows don't seem so drunk, now," Iron Horse said. "It must have been an act."

"So they could drunkenly gun down a lawman," Clint added. "What do you think, Sheriff?"

"I think that's it," Iron Horse said. "Well, if you came here to gun down a lawman, you might as well do it."

"Take the one on the left," Clint told the Apache.

The three men stared at Iron Horse and Clint, licked their lips, and then went for their guns.

Chapter Seventeen

Clint knew they would draw, because they had been hired to do so. Hired guns had no choice but to do their jobs.

Iron Horse drew his gun, and Clint felt sure the lawman would be able to handle one man. These men may have been hired for the guns, but it was for their willingness to use them, not their abilities with them. None of them cleared leather before Iron Horse shot the one on his left, and Clint fired twice, killing the other two.

Clint would have liked to take one of them alive, but with hired men there was no taking any chances. Trying to only wound one. He might have gotten off a lucky shot.

All three men fell dead to the floor.

It was quiet in the room.

"All right," Iron Horse said, holstering his gun. "It's all over. I'll need some of you men to take these bodies out."

Clint ejected his empty shells, reloaded and holstered his weapon.

"No one moved."

"Al!" Daisy called.

The bartender went into action.

"Come on," he said, rushing around the bar. "You, you, and you three, let's go."

Five men moved forward and between them and the bartender, they carried the three men out.

Daisy stepped from the crowd to join Clint and Iron Horse. The others started to go back to their tables, and places at the bar, but gave Clint and Iron Horse a wide berth.

The bartender came back in.

"They're takin' them fellers to the undertaker, Sheriff," he said.

"Thanks, Al."

"Do you really think those men were hired to kill you?" Daisy asked.

"Someone tried to bushwhack us earlier, outside of town," Clint said. "This was a follow-up, I'm sure."

"Well," she said, "you handled it quite well."

"Thank you for trying to help," Iron Horse said.

She looked down. "I was trying to keep blood off my floor."

Clint looked down, as well, saw a few drops.

"Not too bad," he said. "Al moved quickly to get them out of here."

"It's Al's job to move quickly," she said.

"More beer?" Al asked.

"No," Iron Horse said, "I want to check on those bodies at the undertaker's, see if there's anything to tell us who hired them."

"So we'll be going," Clint added.

"Don't forget to come back for that private talk," Daisy told Clint.

"I'll remember," Clint said.

He and Iron Horse left, to the relief of the rest of the customers.

***

Clint watched as Iron Horse went through the dead men's pockets.

"Nothing," Iron Horse said, "not even any money to show how much they were paid." He looked at the undertaker. "They're all yours."

The undertaker nodded.

Clint and Iron Horse left the office and headed toward Iron Horse's house. Both were very alert for another ambush.

When they got to the door Iron Horse asked, "Want to come in?"

"I think I'll go back to The Lady Gay for that quiet talk with Daisy."

"You can tell me about it tomorrow morning," Iron Horse said. "Breakfast at Big Man's?"

"Suits me," Clint said.

"Good night, then."

"Iron Horse," Clint said, as the man opened the door.

"Yes?"

"What they said back there, about a savage being sheriff?"

"It didn't offend me," Iron Horse said. "I'm not that thin-skinned. Good night."

"Good night."

Clint walked back toward the center of town, and The Lady Gay. When he entered, he went right to the bar.

"Back again?" Al asked. "Beer?"

"I'm here to talk with Miss Daisy," Clint said.

"Well, she's up in her room. I'm sure it's okay for you to go up."

"Then I'll take a beer and a champagne with me."

"Comin' up."

Armed with a champagne flute and a chilly mug, he went up the stairs to the second floor and knocked on Daisy's door.

"Come in."

"I'm afraid my hands are full," Clint said.

Daisy opened the door, smiled and said, "Not as full as they're going to be."

Chapter Eighteen

Clint stepped in with the two glasses and Daisy closed the door behind him. She wasn't wearing the yellow gown anymore, but a lavender robe that was belted tightly at the waist. It emphasized her busty build.

"Well," she said, accepting the champagne from him, "what did you find out?"

"Yvette Cormier," he said.

"Ah." She sipped her champagne.

"Is that your real name?"

"Could be," she said. "Have you mentioned it to anyone else?"

"Only the sheriff."

"And the telegraph operator?"

"I doubt anyone in that job retains any knowledge of the telegrams."

"I hope you're right."

"Then it is your real name?"

She sipped her champagne and said, "Drink your beer."

He sipped it, then set it down.

"I want to be sharp when I walk back to the hotel in the dark," he said.

She put her glass down and undid the belt of her robe.

"Who says you'll be walking in the dark?"

The promise of what was beneath her gown and robe was revealed in all its splendor when she shrugged, leaving her naked. But she was much more than splendid.

"You're beautiful," he said.

"Get undressed," she said, "and maybe I'll say the same thing about you."

"Don't you have to work anymore, tonight?" he asked.

"I'm the boss," she said. "I work when I want."

He could feel the heat coming off her naked body.

"What's wrong?" she asked, putting her hands on her hips. "Afraid I'm setting a trap?"

"Could be," he said. "If you are, it's a beauty."

"Look," she said, walking to the door, "I'll lock it." She did so. "And there's no access from the window."

She walked to the bed, pulled down the sheet and sat on it.

"The rest is up to you," she said.

"I suppose it is," he said, and undid his gunbelt.

***

80

Mayor Dandridge entered John Nettles office. The saloon owner looked up from his desk.

"What happened?" he asked.

"Three dead men, over at The Lady Gay."

"Iron Horse?"

"And Clint Adams," Dandridge said. "Both alive."

"I knew he was going to be a problem," Nettles said. "Where are they now?"

"I think Iron Horse is in his house," the mayor said.

"And Adams?"

"He went back to The Lady Gay."

Nettles stood, walked to a sideboard and poured himself a brandy.

"Want one?" he asked.

"Sure."

The mayor sat and Nettles handed him a glass of brandy, then returned to his desk with his own.

"Are you sure Iron Horse won't give up his badge?" Nettles asked.

"Not until he's good and ready."

"And when might that be?"

"Who knows?" Dandridge said. "Maybe not until he finds whoever killed that other Apache, White Horse."

Nettles sipped his drink.

"Well then," he said, "maybe we should make sure he does just that."

***

After hanging his gunbelt on the bedpost, Clint removed his boots and clothes, until he was also naked.

"Well," she said, "it's about time. Come over here."

He walked to the bed and stood in front of her. She ran her hands over his chest, belly, hips, and butt cheeks, then brought them around to concentrate on his cock, which was already hard.

"Very nice," she said, stroking him, fondling him while he ran his hands over the smooth, warm flesh of her back and shoulders, until he reached between them to fondle her large breasts.

Finally, he drew her to her feet so he could hold her in his arms and kiss her, their bodies pressed together. Eventually, they fell onto the bed together, still kissing, this time their legs entwining. She rolled around on the bed for a while, until they finally settled into a position where he was pressing his face between her legs. He worked her into a frenzy with his lips and tongue until her body went taut, and then quivered with waves of pleasure that had her almost in tears . . .

***

"My God!" she breathed moments later, as they lay side-by-side, regaining their breath.

"You see?" she said, then. "No trap, no attack."

"I see that," Clint said. "I mean, no attack, but this could still be a trap."

She rolled onto her side and grasped his semi-hard penis, gently.

"You still think this might be a trap?" she asked, stroking him.

He looked down at her hand and said, "I think I might still need more information."

"I'll see what I can do," she said, sliding down between his legs.

She ran her lips up and down his cock, then used her tongue to wet him thoroughly. When he glistened with her saliva, she opened her mouth and took him inside. She started to suck him slowly, languidly, and he closed his eyes, keeping his hands at his sides. As her tempo increased, accompanied by moans and sighs, he reached for her head and cupped it gently in his hands . . .

Chapter Nineteen

Clint woke the next morning as Daisy slid from the bed and padded naked across the room. When she pulled on her robe, she saw him watching her.

"I'm sorry I woke you," she said.

"That's okay," he said. "I should be getting up, anyway. Where are you off to today?"

"Some shopping, some business," she said. "Will I see you tonight?"

"I'm sure you will," Clint said. "That is, unless another bushwhacker is successful."

"Let's hope not," she said, sitting in front of her dressing table.

Clint got to his feet, and she watched him in the mirror as he got dressed.

"So, what's the verdict?" she asked.

"Verdict?" he asked, strapping on his guns.

She turned and asked, "Was this a trap?"

"Oh definitely," Clint said. He walked to her, bent and kissed her. "And expertly laid. See you tonight."

He left and headed for Big Man's.

***

When he entered, Iron Horse was sitting there with a cup of coffee waiting for him. There was no one else in the place.

"Good morning," the lawman greeted.

"Good morning," Clint said, sitting opposite him.

"How did it go with Daisy last night?" Iron Horse asked. "Did she admit to being Yvette?"

"She said it was possible," Clint replied, "but never admitted it, right out."

"Breakfast, gentlemen?"

They both turned their eyes toward the kitchen door. Little Deer stood there, waiting for their reply.

"Where's Big Man?" Iron Horse asked.

"Papa's not feeling well, today," she said. "I told him I would handle breakfast."

Clint noticed that when her father wasn't there, she seemed older, more of a woman than a girl.

"Bring us whatever you're making," Clint said. "I'm sure it'll be fine."

"I'll do that," she said, "as soon as I get you a cup of coffee, Mr. Adams."

"Thank you."

She went into the kitchen.

"She seems . . . different," Clint said.

"She puts on a little girl act for her father," Iron Horse said. "Because he wants her to stay a little girl. But when he's not around . . ."

"I get it," Clint said. "And you and she have been . . . together?"

"We have," Iron Horse said. "But only when Big Man's not around."

"And if Big Man found out?"

"He would kill me."

"What if you married her?" Clint asked.

"That would be different," Iron Horse admitted. "But I am not looking to get married. I am going to the mountains, remember? That is no place for a girl."

"Probably not," Clint said, "although I'm sure there are mountain girls."

Little Deer came out with Clint's coffee and said, "The food will be ready, soon."

"Thank you, Lisa," Iron Horse said.

She smiled and returned to the kitchen.

"Now," Iron Horse said, "tell me about you and Miss Daisy—or Miss Yvette."

Chapter Twenty

Little Deer—or Lisa—brought out a very normal looking breakfast of ham-and-eggs, and biscuits. However, it tasted better than any ham-and-egg breakfast Clint had ever had.

"I will bring more coffee," she said.

"So?" Iron Horse said. "What now? Are you convinced that Miss Daisy is not our culprit?"

"Pretty convinced."

"Then who?"

"We may have to wait for someone to try again," Clint said, "and then try to take them alive for questioning."

"Are you willing to stay around that long?" Iron Horse asked.

"I don't think it'll be that long," Clint said. "Two attempts in one day. Whoever it is, they're getting reckless."

"You're right," Iron Horse said.

"I suggest we finish breakfast, get ourselves a couple of chairs and sit outside your office."

"Putting ourselves out there as targets?" Iron Horse said. "Have you done that before?"

"Several times."

"And it has worked?"

"A time or two," Clint said. "It might take a few days, but no longer."

"We can still make rounds," Iron Horse said.

"Sure," Clint said, "that may be when they make their next move."

"They should hire better guns than those three last night," Iron Horse said.

"Or," Clint amended, "they better not."

***

After breakfast they left and went to the sheriff's office.

"Tell me about your mayor," Clint said, as they sat down.

"What about him?"

"Is he ready for you to give up the badge?"

"I think so," Iron Horse said. "He is happy with the job I have done, but now I believe I may be in his way. Yes, he has suggested I step aside."

"And you told him no," Clint said. "To what ends would he go to get you to leave?"

"You mean, would the mayor hire guns?" Iron Horse asked. "To tell you the truth, I don't know."

"What if we pressed him?" Clint asked. "He didn't strike me as a man who has a lot of sand."

"I think he would need someone else behind him," Iron Horse said.

"Somebody in town," Clint said. "Or a rancher?"

"And that puts us right back to where we started," Iron Horse said. "I must tell you, I am not comfortable putting myself out there just . . . sitting."

"Hey," Clint said, "you're the sheriff. Come up with a better idea."

"We were going to check the mercantile for sales of forty-four forty ammunition."

"Fine," Clint said, "let's do that. But just remember, whether we're sitting outside there or walking the street, we're out there. Somebody is going to try again."

"I prefer they come after us head on like last night, and not from ambush."

"I agree," Clint said.

They left the office and headed for the mercantile store. When they entered, the man behind the counter seemed surprised.

"Sheriff," he said, "what can I do for you?"

"Why so surprised, Mr. Hayes?" Iron Horse asked.

"I'm not surprised," the man said. "Just a little . . . uncomfortable. I heard about what happened in the saloon last night. I don't really want to be around when bullets start flying."

"Then I'll just ask you a question and we'll be on our way," Iron Horse said. "Forty-four forties, has anyone made a large purchase, recently?"

"Forty-four forties," Hayes repeated, thinking. "Good ammo, fits a rifle or a pistol."

"I know that," Iron Horse said. "I want to know if you have sold anyone a large amount of them."

"Not that I can think of," Hayes said. He grabbed some boxes from behind him and set them on the counter. "As you can see, I have plenty. They're popular."

"That they are," Clint said. "If anyone comes in for some, would you let the sheriff know?"

"I sure will," Hayes said, replacing the boxes on the shelf. "Uh, anything else?"

"No," Iron Horse said. "That will be all. Thank you."

Just outside the store, Clint asked, "What about storekeepers?"

"What about them?"

"Any of them want you gone?"

"No," Iron Horse said. "When I set down the law against guns in town to keep those drunk ranch hands out, it didn't really affect any of their businesses. In fact, they like that I make my rounds each night and check their doors. I would have to say the business owners are the only ones who don't want me to resign."

"I've got an idea," Clint said.

"What?"

"Let's go to your office and talk about it."

Chapter Twenty-One

"Close the saloons?" Iron Horse repeated.

"That's what I said," Clint replied.

"Why?"

"You don't just want to sit around, you want to take action," Clint said. "What other action can we take?"

"You think this will force Daisy and Nettles' hand?" the Apache lawman asked.

"I think it'll force *somebody's* hand," Clint said. "Maybe one of them, maybe the mayor, maybe just some cowboy because you're taking his whiskey away from him."

"I don't think a cowboy will try to kill me for taking away his whiskey," Iron Horse said.

"I don't, either," Clint said, "but you've already outlawed their guns in town. Taking their whiskey might be the last straw."

"But if it's just some thirsty cowboy, how does that help us?"

"It doesn't," Clint said. "At least we'll be making a move."

Iron Horse sat back in the chair and thought it over.

"I have not done that before," he said, finally. "How do I go about it?"

"You wait until each saloon is as full as can be, then walk in and announce that the place is closed."

"For how long?"

"Indefinitely," Clint said.

Iron Horse frowned.

"No one will like that."

"Then we can go back to our other plan," Clint said. "Sit out front and wait."

"*I* do not like that one," Iron Horse said.

"Well, I'm open to suggestions."

"I think we should go into The Lady Gay tonight and see if anyone there recognized the three men from last night."

Clint's eyebrows went up.

"Okay, that's a good idea," he said, "but what if we come up empty?"

"Then we'll go with your idea," Iron Horse said. "We'll close the saloons and see if that shakes anybody up."

In point of fact, Clint didn't much like the idea of sitting out front and waiting. It seemed to him he had done that too many times already. But once or twice it had brought somebody out of the woodwork. Still, it was a fairly stagnant way of doing things.

"All right, then," Iron Horse said. "We might as well make some afternoon rounds and see if anybody takes a shot at us."

Clint sighed and said, "That's a way to go, too."

***

When the mayor entered John Nettles' office, he did not look happy.

"I don't like being summoned," he said.

"It's better than me being seen going into your office," Nettles said.

The mayor sat.

"All right, so what's on your mind?"

"I sent a couple of telegrams."

"And?"

"We should have some action in the next couple of days."

"The man who shot that Indian deputy?"

"He's the only one who's been successful, so far," Nettles said. "I sent for him and told him to bring some help."

"Another ambush?" the mayor asked, with a look of distaste.

"You know," Nettles said, "part of our problem is you have a soft spot for that Apache lawman of yours."

"He's done a good job for six months," Dandridge argued.

"And now we need him to go away," Nettles said. "Permanently."

Dandridge frowned, but didn't argue the point.

***

Clint and Iron Horse walked the town, looking for trouble of any kind. A couple of storekeepers sweeping up in front of their doors gave the sheriff a nod, but for the most part the street was deserted.

At one point, though, they were walking across the street from The Nebraska Saloon and Iron Horse grabbed Clint's arm, pulling him into a doorway.

"I see him," Clint said.

Coming out of the Nebraska was the mayor. He turned his head both ways, as if checking to see if anyone saw him, then hurried away.

"What do you suppose that was about?"

"I would say a drink, but it's early," Iron Horse said. "And the mayor is not a heavy drinker."

"So what would he have to do with John Nettles?" Clint wondered.

"There is one way to find out," Iron Horse said.

They stepped from the doorway and crossed the street.

Chapter Twenty-Two

The bartender was wiping the bar as they entered. He stopped and stared at them.

"Not open, yet," he said.

"Really?" Clint said. "Because we just saw the mayor come out of here."

"He's the mayor," the bartender said, as if that explained everything.

"We would like to see Mr. Nettles," Iron Horse said.

"And there's no need to announce us, this time." Clint added.

He and the sheriff headed to the back of the room.

"Hey, wait—" the bartender started, but they ignored him.

When they reached Nettles' office door, they opened it without knocking and went in. The man looked up from his desk in surprise.

"Well," he said, "nice of you to knock."

"We just saw the mayor leaving here, Mr. Nettles," Clint said.

"We wondered what business he had with you," Iron Horse said.

Nettles sat back.

"Well, as you know, Sheriff, I'm on the town council," he said. "The mayor had some council business to discuss. I'm sure you'll find he's talked or is talking to other members."

"About what?" Iron Horse asked.

"I'm sorry," Nettles said, "that's council business. If you're interested, ask the mayor and see if he tells you."

Clint knew that Iron Horse was itching to tell Nettles his place was closed, but they had agreed to do it at the height of business that night.

"Very well," Iron Horse said, "I will do that."

"And please close the door on your way out," Nettles said, turning his attention back to his desk.

Clint and Iron Horse left, the Apache slamming the door behind him.

"I do not like that man."

"I don't blame you," Clint said.

They stopped outside the saloon and looked up and down the empty street.

"I'm curious," Clint said, then, "who else is on the council? Daisy?"

"No," Iron Horse said. "She is a business owner. But they will not allow a woman to sit on the council. Several of the other business owners—including Mr. Hayes from the mercantile, are on it."

"Let's check in with Hayes," Clint suggested.

"Fine."

***

"No," Hayes said, "the mayor hasn't been in here to-day. Why do you ask?"

"We understood he was conducting some town council business this morning," Clint said.

"Council business is only conducted during a meetin'," Hayes commented. "He shouldn't be discussin' it outside of City Hall."

"I guess the mayor makes his own rules," Clint said.

Hayes frowned.

"He's not usually that aggressive."

"Then maybe we were wrong," Clint said. "It's just that we saw him coming out of The Nebraska Saloon. Mr. Nettles is on the council, right?"

Hayes made a face.

"He thinks he runs the council," Hayes said. "If he and the mayor are takin' business between them, the other council members ain't gonna like it."

"Well," Clint said, "we weren't looking to cause trouble. We were just asking. Good day, Mr. Hayes."

Clint and Iron Horse left the merchant shaking his head.

"I think we may have started some trouble for Mr. Mayor," Clint said, outside.

"I do not mind that at all," Iron Horse said.

***

They completed Iron Horse's rounds and returned to the sheriff's office.

"That was pretty useless," Iron Horse said.

"Not really," Clint said. "We might have stirred some trouble up in the town council. If the mayor and Nettles are planning something, they might have some explaining to do."

"Mr. Hayes said the mayor's not that aggressive," Iron Horse said, "but Nettles is."

"Well," Clint said, "let's see what Mr. Nettles does after you announce tonight that his place is closed indefinitely."

"Do we need to bother closing The Lady Gay?" Iron Horse wondered.

"We're not only targeting Nettles," Clint reminded him. "We might manage to push somebody who sits in The Lady Gay into action."

"How much action could we hope to see from somebody who sits in The Lady Gay and drinks?" Iron Horse asked.

"You know," Clint said, "if you hadn't outlawed guns in the hands of drunks, we might be seeing more action in town."

"If we put guns back into the hands of drunks," Iron Horse said, "we might see more action than we could handle."

Chapter Twenty-Three

Iron Horse managed to find a deck of cards in his desk, and they whiled away the afternoon playing poker and telling stories. Clint didn't usually like talking about his past, but Iron Horse started telling tales about his life in the East, so Clint started sharing, as well. As it turned out, an Apache living in Philadelphia had a lot to say about some of those high-toned society women and how curious they were about "savage men."

"Seems like you were always defending yourself against amorous women, or belligerent men," Clint observed.

"Yes," Iron Horse, "but here it is only the men."

"Don't forget Little Deer."

"She is a lovely girl," Iron Horse said, "but I do not want Big Man to become one of those bad-tempered men I must defend myself against."

"I can't blame you for that," Clint said. "He's a pow-erful looking man."

"You have had your share of experiences, with wom-en and men," Iron Horse observed.

"Yes," Clint said, "luckily most of the women didn't have guns."

Clint turned and looked at the window.

"The saloons should be in full swing," he commented.

Iron Horse put down the cards and stood.

"Might as well get this done," he said. "We should be glad the drunks don't have guns tonight."

"It's a good thing the ranchers are keeping their men out of town," Clint said, as they went out the door.

"There are other towns they can terrorize with their guns," Iron Horse said. "Most of the ranchers are rich and arrogant, but still law-abiding."

As they approached the center of town where the two saloons stood across from each other Iron Horse said, "Let's go to the Nebraska first."

"You're the boss," Clint said.

They entered the Nebraska, found it crowded. The empty tables and places at the bar reflected the missing ranch hands from surrounding spreads, who had been restricted from town by Iron Horse.

Standing just inside the batwing doors, Clint said, "I guess this is as busy as it's going to get."

"Can I have everyone's attention, please!" Iron Horse shouted.

Most of the customers either didn't hear him or ignored him.

Rather than take his gun out and fire it, Iron Horse walked to a nearby table, grabbed an empty beer pitcher and threw it to the floor, shattering it. The sound silenced the room and attracted everyone's attention.

"Thank you," Iron Horse said. "As of now, this establishment is closed, indefinitely. I want all of you to go on home."

Everyone reacted.

"What the—" one man said.

"Is he kiddin'?" another asked.

"What's goin' on?" a third asked.

Other similar comments were expressed, but Iron Horse raised his voice and said, "Go on home . . . now!"

As men began getting to their feet and moving slowly to the door, the bartender came around.

"What's goin' on, Sheriff?" he demanded.

"You heard me," Iron Horse said. "You're closed."

"You can't do this."

"I just did."

"Mr. Nettles ain't gonna like this."

"He can register his complaints with me any time," Iron Horse said.

But at that moment the door in the back wall opened and John Nettles came out. When he saw everyone filing out, he rushed toward the front.

"What in hell's going on?" he demanded.

"The sheriff's closin' us down, Boss," the bartender said.

"What's the meaning of this?" Nettles demanded of Iron Horse.

"Just what your bartender said," Iron Horse replied. "I'm shutting you down."

"Why? For what reason?"

"Too many drunk customers."

"What?" Nettles asked. "Look, you overstepped yourself with that no-guns-in-town rule, but we let that go. But this, this is too much. The council won't stand for it."

"Then take it up at the next council meeting," Iron Horse said. "As of now, you're closed."

Iron Horse turned and walked out. Nettles turned to look at Clint.

"He's out of his mind," he said.

Clint shrugged and said, "He's the law."

"Well, what about The Lady Gay?"

"We're going across the street next," Clint assured him. "Nobody's picking on you, Nettles."

As Clint turned to leave Nettles shouted, "We'll see about this!"

Chapter Twenty-Four

They went through the same thing across the street, minus the smashed glass pitcher. When Iron Horse shouted, the piano stopped, and everyone turned to listen.

"This establishment is closed!" Iron Horse said.

"Sheriff," Al, the bartender called, "what's this about?"

"Just what I said, Al," Iron Horse replied. "You're closed. Everyone go home!"

Customers grumbled about it, but they all headed for the door, giving Iron Horse dirty looks as they went by.

"Miss Daisy's not gonna like this," Al said.

"She can come and complain to me," Iron Horse said. "Or talk to the mayor. I understand there may be a town council meeting about this."

Daisy didn't put in an appearance, so Clint and Iron Horse turned and left. Al closed and locked the doors behind them.

"Is there any place else in town a man can get a drink?" Clint asked.

"When the mercantile opens they can buy a bottle of whiskey there," Iron Horse replied. "I don't know if we want to close the mercantile."

"We can tell Mr. Hayes not to sell any whiskey," Clint suggested.

"Good idea," Iron Horse said. "We can do that in the morning. For now, let's go back to the office and see if we get any complaints."

***

They sat in the sheriff's office for several hours before deciding to pack it in.

"I guess nothing will happen til morning," Clint observed.

"Probably not," Iron Horse said. "I'm sure we will hear from the mayor, or someone on the town council."

"Don't forget, Mr. Hayes might raise a ruckus with them," Clint said.

"True," Iron Horse said.

They left the office and locked the door, then started walking toward the sheriff's house. It was dark as they approached, but they stayed very alert.

"You have ears like an Apache," Iron Horse said. "Better than mine. Hear anything?"

"Nothing," Clint said.

They stopped in front of the sheriff's small house.

"You don't think they would try for me here, do you?" Iron Horse said.

"Well," Clint said. "On the trail and in the saloon. I'd expect something in the street next, but there's nothing wrong with being careful."

They approached the front door together, which Iron Horse unlocked with a key. Before entering Clint went to a front window and peered in, but it was too dark to see anything.

"I could go to the back," Clint said.

"There is no back door," Iron Horse told him. "If you have a feeling, you could check a back window."

"Actually," Clint said, "I don't feel a thing."

"Then we can go in."

Iron House opened the door and swung it wide, then lit a match before entering. While Clint watched, he walked to an oil lamp on a table and touched the match to it. The room lit up with a yellowish glow and Clint stepped in. He saw a table, two chairs, a cot and a pot-bellied stove.

"This is all the town gave you?"

"I am an Apache," Iron Horse said. "This is all I need."

Clint realized the furnishings were the lawman's choice.

"Well," Clint said, "it looks like you're alone and safe."

"I think I will turn in," Iron Horse said. "Watch yourself on the way back to your hotel."

"I'll be extra alert," Clint said. "Big Man's in the morning?"

"That sounds fine."

"Good night, then."

Clint left and walked to his hotel without any incident. He passed both saloons, quiet and dark. When he entered the lobby, he noticed the clerk staring at him nervously. Upstairs, he approached his room as silently as he could, pressed his ear to the door. Unlike the sheriff's house, his senses were warning him that someone was inside. The nervous desk clerk confirmed it for him.

He used his key to unlock the door, then swung it open violently and crouched down, gun in hand.

"Oh!" Daisy DuValier gasped from her seat on the bed. "You startled me."

"Can't be too careful," he said. He stepped inside, looked behind the door, then closed it and holstered his gun.

"How did you know I was here?" she asked.

"I knew someone was here," he said. "The fact that it's you is a nice surprise."

She stood up, straightened the simple grey dress she was wearing, and approached him.

"How pleasant?" she asked.

Chapter Twenty-Five

Clint showed her how pleasant it was by roughly removing her clothes, tossing her, naked, onto the bed before removing his own clothes and joining her. He fucked her good and hard leaving them both gasping for air when he was done. This was totally different from the gentle lovemaking they had shared before.

"I think you're trying to kill me," she said.

"If that was true," he said, "It would be suicide and murder."

"Or," she said, propping herself up on one elbow, "you're trying to make me feel better for closing me down tonight."

"We couldn't very well close down The Nebraska without shutting you down, as well. Make him think it's routine. But the truth is we wanted to put some pressure on him to make a move."

"If, in fact, it's him who's trying to kill the two of you."

"Yes," Clint said, "This should force his hand."

"And if it's not him?"

"Then maybe somebody else will take offense and make a try," Clint said.

"And you'll be ready for them?"

"Yes."

"You know," she said, "if it is Nettles, then the mayor's involved. And probably some of the town council."

"We figured that," Clint said. "Dandridge couldn't get Iron Horse to give up his badge, so maybe he wants to force the issue."

"You left the sheriff alone at his house?"

"Yes."

"Are you sure he's safe?"

"Safer than if he was in his office," Clint said. "Backshooters and bushwhackers may not even know where he lives."

"And you? Here?"

"They might try something," Clint said, reaching out and touching his gun, which was on the bedpost, "but this is never far."

"I've noticed," she said. "Even in bed."

"Tell me something, Daisy."

"Yes."

"Why wouldn't a smart woman like you force her way onto the town council?"

"I don't want to make waves, darling," she said. "Remember?"

"Yvette?"

"You wouldn't happen to have any champagne here, would you?"

Instead of answering, he gathered her into his arms, and she laughed.

***

Clint watched as Daisy/Yvette dressed.

"You're a passionate man," she said. "You tore my dress."

"You're lucky I didn't tear it to pieces," he said. "You bring that out in a man."

She walked to the bed, bent and kissed him.

"I'm sorry I can't stay the night."

"Well, as you said, somebody might try for me here. I'd rather you weren't around if that happens."

"Make sure you lock the door and the windows," she said.

"There's no access from the windows," Clint said. "And I always lock my door."

"Good night, then," she said. "Oh, when do you think I can reopen?"

"I'll let you know."

"Oh well," she said, with a sigh, "I can use the day off." She touched her dress. "I need to shop."

She left the room. Clint padded naked to the door and locked it, then went back to bed.

***

Sometime later he was wakened by a noise. He stayed still and listened, thought he could hear someone in the hall. It could have been another guest returning to their room. He sat up so he could reach his gun easily. If someone wanted to try for him, they would have to kick the door open.

He rose and, gun in hand, went to the door. He opened it a crack, looked out, then swung it open wider and stepped out to look both ways. Nothing. He closed the door and locked it, again.

He slept fitfully the rest of the might, ready for anything.

Chapter Twenty-Six

They met again at Big Man's for breakfast. The Sioux was there this time, and Little Deer was back in the kitchen. Without a word he brought them each a cup of coffee.

When he carried breakfast in, he glared at them, as if he suspected them of doing something to his daughter. Breakfast was more in keeping with an Indian meal. Iron Horse told Clint it was called "sofgee."

"It is corn porridge," the Apache lawman said, "and johnny cakes."

Clint preferred the breakfast Little Deer had given them the day before, but he ate what was in front of him.

"What do you think?" Iron Horse asked.

"It's fine," Clint said.

Iron Horse laughed.

"I thought I heard someone last night in the hall outside my room," Clint said. "Either they changed their minds, or it was just another guest returning to their room."

"That's funny," Iron Horse said. "I thought I heard someone outside my house, but when I got up and looked, nobody was there."

"Maybe we're getting jumpy," Clint suggested.

"Maybe we are just staying alert. Did you see Miss Daisy last night?"

"I did, on the way back to my hotel."

"Was she upset?"

"She was very understanding," Clint said. "She knew we were trying to push someone into a move."

"And did she admit to being Miss Yvette?"

"Not exactly," Clint said, "but she did say she wants to keep her head low."

"So she owns a saloon?"

"Maybe she just doesn't know what else to do," Clint said. "I asked why she didn't push herself onto the council. That's when she said she's laying low."

They finished their breakfast without seeing Big Man again.

"Did you see the look he gave us?" Clint asked.

"I know," Iron Horse said. "He is not a man to cross, Clint."

"I have no intention of crossing him."

Once outside Iron Horse said, "Let's go and see Mr. Hayes. Tell him he cannot sell any liquor for now."

"And let's find out if he talked to any of the town council members, about the mayor and Nettles."

They walked to the mercantile, encountering one or two people, but the streets were largely deserted. When they entered Hayes was alone, standing behind the counter.

"Ah, Sheriff," he said. "You were wrong, you know."

"Was I?" Iron Horse asked. "About what?"

"The mayor wasn't discussing town council business with Nettles," Hayes said. "Not at all."

"What was it, then?" Clint asked.

"Private," Hayes said, "it was private."

"And who told you this?"

"The mayor, himself."

"Did you buy it?" Clint asked.

"What? Well, yes, why shouldn't I believe him?"

"Just wondering," Clint said.

"Mr. Hayes," Iron Horse said, "I closed down the saloons last night."

"You did?" Hayes asked. "That must've upset Nettles." The man looked happy at that prospect.

"It did. But now I have to upset you," the sheriff said.

"What? How?"

"I'm afraid you can't sell any liquor—at least, for the time being."

"So the whole town is dry?"

"Yes."

Hayes thought a minute, then said, "I guess I can't argue with that, if it extends to everyone."

"It does."

"Well," Hayes said, shrugging, "okay, then. Anythin' else?"

"No, nothing," Iron Horse said. "Thanks a lot for understanding."

"I'm afraid I don't understand, Sheriff," Hayes said. "But I'm not gonna argue with ya."

"Have a good day, Mr. Hayes."

"You too, gents."

Clint and Iron Horse left the store, stopped just outside. Clint scanned the street, the windows and roof tops across the way.

"Nothing," he said to Iron Horse. "Nobody's looking down their sights at us."

"Not yet, anyway," Iron Horse said.

"How'd you like to push the mayor, a bit?" Clint asked.

Iron Horse shrugged and said, "Why not?"

Chapter Twenty-Seven

The mayor looked up from his desk when they entered and frowned.

"What do you want?" he asked Iron Horse.

"That's no way to talk to your town sheriff," Clint commented.

"I'm sorry," Dandridge said, "I'm very busy. What can I do for you?"

"I suppose you heard I closed down the saloons," Iron Horse said.

"I did hear that," Dandridge said. "I don't understand it, but you're the law."

That attitude surprised both Clint and Iron Horse.

"I expected something different," Iron Horse said. "Didn't your friend, Nettles, come by and complain?"

"He did," the mayor said, "and I told him the same thing. You are the law—at least, for now."

That was more like it, Clint thought.

"For the foreseeable future, *I* think," Clint said. "Thanks, Mr. Mayor."

He tugged at Iron Horse's arm, and they left the office.

"He's playing games, now," Clint said, outside.

"I am not playing games," Iron Horse said. "What we have to do now is your idea."

"Which one?"

"Sitting in front of my office and waiting," Iron Horse said. "Eventually, someone will come."

"When they come, they usually bring help," Clint told him.

"That is all right," Iron Horse said. "You and me, we can handle whatever comes."

"I hope you're right," Clint said.

"You know I am right," Iron Horse said, "or you would have left town and never agreed to help me."

Clint shrugged.

"Then let's go and sit," he said. "What do you want to do while we sit? Whittle?"

***

While they sat, they talked.

For some of the time they just remained silent.

There was no whittling.

By the end of the day, no riders had appeared.

"What if they came in on foot?" Iron Horse suggested, "went into the Nebraska by a back door?"

"Could be," Clint said. "If that's the case they'll be on the street soon."

"I am getting hungry," Iron Horse said.

"I don't want to go back to Big Man's," Clint said. "Not if he's going to give us some more sofgee."

"That's only for breakfast."

"Well, he's also not in a very good mood," Clint said. "How about some sandwiches from the café. We can go get them and bring them back here to eat."

"Sounds like a good idea."

They both rose and walked down the street to the small café. As they entered, they saw it was empty. A white-haired waiter came from the kitchen.

"We're getting ready to close, gents."

"Can you fix us two sandwiches to take with us?" Iron Horse asked. "We'll eat them at my office."

"Sure, Sheriff," the waiter said. "Chicken okay with you?"

"That would be fine."

"Won't be a minute," the waiter said.

Clint kept his eyes trained on the street while Iron Horse stood further inside. Finally, the waiter came out with two wrapped sandwiches and handed them to the lawman.

"What do I owe you?" Iron Horse asked.

"It's on the house for the law, Sheriff," the waiter said. "Some folks in this town like what you've done with the place."

"Thank you," Iron Horse said. "I appreciate that."

He stepped outside and stood next to Clint.

"Anything?" he asked.

"Not a soul. What've you got?"

"Chicken."

"That'll do," Clint said. "Let's get back to our chairs so we can eat."

Chapter Twenty-Eight

John Nettles entered a curtained back room that he used for private poker games. The four men seated at the round, green felt table looked up at him.

"About time," a tall man named Blaisdell said. "Where are our drinks?"

"Coming," Nettles said. He looked across the table at the man farthest from him. He was a big, flat-cheeked, long-haired Comanche named Spotted Dog. Nettles wondered if the smattering of spots on his face had anything to do with his name?

"Glad to see you brought him back with you," Nettles said. "He's the only one who accomplished anything when he killed that other Apache."

"His name was White Horse," Spotted Dog said. "He was a good man."

The bartender came in with a tray of drinks— whiskey for the three white men, and a beer for Spotted Dog.

"This is Pete, and this is Lee."

Nettles ignored the men. He'd never be able to tell them from a dozen others. They looked just like a couple of ranch hands.

He sat and regarded Blaisdell.

"Are you prepared for this?" he asked.

"Goin' up against the Gunsmith?" Blaisdell asked. "I've been waitin' all my life."

Blaisdell did not yet look forty.

"I want him gone," Nettles said. "Once he is then we can work on the sheriff."

"Iron Horse," Spotted Dog said. "He is a good man."

"We'll take them both at the same time," Blaisdell said. "Easier that way."

"They're sitting in front of the sheriff's office right now, eating."

"It is bad to kill a man while he is eating," Spotted Dog said.

Nettles looked at him.

"Is that an old Comanche wives' tale?" he asked.

Spotted Dog stared at Nettles.

"It is a bad thing."

"Don't worry," Blaisdell told the Comanche. "We can wait." He looked at the bartender. "We'll need more drinks."

The bartender looked at his boss, who nodded.

"Three whiskeys and a beer?"

"Just the whiskey," Blaisdell said. "Spotted Dog only needs one beer."

The bartender nodded and left.

"Half up front," Blaisdell said to Nettles.

The saloon owner nodded, reached into his jacket pocket and came out with a stack of bills, which he dropped onto the table. One of the white men reached for it, but yanked his hand back in time to avoid Spotted Dog's knife, which impaled itself in the tabletop.

"Spotted Dog doesn't like anybody touchin' the money," Blaisdell said, as he reclaimed his knife.

Nettles stood up.

"We want this done before tomorrow night," he said. "I need to reopen by then."

"It'll get done," Blaisdell told him.

"There are two rooms upstairs for you," Nettles said. "If you want a girl, let me know."

"That won't be necessary," Blaisdell said.

"Aw, boss," Pete whined.

"No girls!" Spotted Dog snapped.

"Tell your trained Comanche to take it easy," Lee said.

"I'd be careful if I was you," Blaisdell said. "He ain't so tamed."

As Nettles left, Pete and Lee stared at Spotted Dog, who sipped his beer.

***

Clint and Iron Horse sat in their chairs and ate their sandwiches.

"These are good," Clint commented. "Chicken *and* vegetables."

"They did not charge me," Iron Horse said. "The waiter said there were people in town who appreciated what I did."

"Lucky for us," Clint said. He swallowed and washed it down with a sip of coffee Iron Horse had fetched from inside.

"We don't want to sit out here after dark," Clint said. "We can come back in the morning."

"Another night of staying alert," Iron Horse said.

"They'll do something soon," Clint said. "I don't think this town wants the saloons closed for very long."

"You are saying you think it is Nettles?"

"And the mayor," Clint said. "They want you out."

"Not the ranchers?"

"I think if it was one of the ranchers, he'd be sending a bunch of his men to town with guns. When you tried to take them away . . . well, there's safety in numbers."

"Well," Iron Horse said, "your feelings have been right, so far."

Iron Horse took the paper their sandwiches were wrapped in and, taking his own, took them inside to dispose of them. Then he refilled their coffee mugs and took his seat again.

"Let's give it another half hour," he said. "I have an itch of my own."

"About what?"

"I feel like we're being watched," Iron Horse said. "Not by anyone with a gun, but simply watched."

"You're probably right," Clint said. "There could be any number of citizens watching us from windows, waiting for something to happen."

"You should have seen this street when I first got here," Iron Horse said. "It was busy with people, horses, wagons, buckboards. The streets were covered with wheel ruts."

"And drunks with guns," Clint reminded him.

"Yes," Iron Horse said, "riding up and down, shooting out windows."

"I prefer this," Clint said.

"So do I," Iron Horse said. "But once I leave, things will go back to the way they were."

"You think so?"

"Unless they hire a real lawman," Iron Horse added. "He could keep things down to a low roar."

"That might be part of their plan," Clint said. "New name, new law."

"But they would have to bring someone in from outside," Iron Horse said. "I still don't believe anyone local would want the job."

"Well," Clint said, "that's going to be somebody else's problem, isn't it?"

"Yes," Iron Horse said. "Once I have found White Horse's killer, I am finished with this town."

Chapter Twenty-Nine

Blaisdell dismissed Pete and Lee, telling them to remain available.

"That means saloons, and no whorehouses," he told them.

"The saloons are closed down, Boss," Pete said.

"Then stay in your room, upstairs."

"Right," Lee said.

"And no whores!" Blasdell snapped, as they left the back room.

That left Blaisdell with Spotted Dog, who still had some of his beer left.

"What do you know about Iron Horse?" he asked.

"He is a good man," Spotted Dog said.

"You said that about White Horse."

"He was also a good man."

"Well," Blaisdell said, "you killed White Horse. Are you willing to kill Iron horse?"

"I have killed many good men." A brief smile crossed his granite hard face. "I am a better man."

"That's what I wanted to hear."

"And you will kill the Gunsmith?" Spotted Dog asked.

"Of course."

"Face-to-face?"

"I'm thinkin' about that," Blaisdell said.

"I have to kill Iron Horse face-to-face?"

"You can do it any way you see fit," Blaisdell said. "Just do it tomorrow."

Spotted Dog nodded.

"It will be done."

"With no saloons open, I suppose we'd better turn in," Blaisdell said. "I think we're sharin' a room."

Spotted Dog made a face.

"I do not like sharing a room with a white man."

"That's fine," Blaisdell said. "I'll check with Nettles and get myself another room."

Spotted Dog nodded, stood up, finished his beer, and left.

Blaisdell figured Iron Horse was as good as dead. He didn't know who Nettles had used on his last two attempts, but the third was going to be successful.

Now it was up to him to finish the Gunsmith. And for that he needed a girl. A soft, willing woman always helped him when he had to think. That was something else he was going to ask Nettles about.

He finished his drink and went to find his host.

***

"I think," Iron Horse said, "it might be a good idea if both of us spent the night here."

Clint touched the wall behind them and said, "In jail?"

"Since we both felt something last night, it might be smart for us to watch each other's back all night."

"I agree," Clint said. "Do you need anything from your house?"

"No," Iron Horse said. "What about you? Something from your hotel room?"

"No," Clint said. "I think we have everything we need here. Our guns." Clint touched his Peacemaker.

"And coffee," Iron Horse said.

"Exactly."

"Then we might as well go inside," Iron Horse said. "If you are right, tomorrow should be a big day."

"Let's hope so," Clint said. "The quiet in this town is starting to get on my nerves."

"The quiet is the one thing in this town that does not bother me," Iron Horse said, as they stood.

"Must be the Apache in you," Clint said.

"Yes," Iron Horse said. "Even in Philadelphia I noticed the white man's need for . . . noise."

***

Blaisdell waited in the room Nettles had provided for him. It was away from the room his men, Pete and Lee, occupied, so they wouldn't see him with a girl.

Blaisdell looked around the room. There was a bottle of brandy and two glasses on a table, and the blanket and sheets on the bed were turned down. Blaisdell was bare-chested and barefoot, while still wearing his trousers. Those would come off later.

When the knock came on the door Blaisdell opened it.

"I have what you asked for," Nettles said.

"Good," Blaisdell said. He walked to the bed and sat on it.

Nettles smiled and stepped aside. The girl entered, long darkhaired, bare shoulders beneath a colorful blanket. Dark eyes and a lovely face. And young, very young.

"Will she do?"

"That depends," Blaisdell said.

Nettles looked at the girl. She smiled and dropped the blanket to the floor. Beneath it she was naked, sleek, with pert breasts tipped with dark nipples.

"Yes," Blaisdell said, "she'll do."

"Then enjoy your evening," Nettles said, and left.

"Tell me," Blaisdell said, "what's your name?"

"Little Deer," the girl said, "but you can call me Lisa."

Chapter Thirty

There were two cells in the cellblock, which suited Clint and Iron Horse just fine. They each claimed one, then went back out to the office for some more coffee.

"The door's locked, the windows are closed and curtained," Iron Horse told him.

The Apache lawman sat behind his desk, while Clint sat across from him.

"Do you mind?" he asked, putting his feet up on the desk.

"Not at all." They sipped their coffee. "When do you think we can expect something?"

"This town already feels like a tinder box," Clint said. "I think those three drunks were meant to be the lighted fuse."

"And they failed."

"Which means somebody'll be in a hurry to get it done," Clint said. "I expect trouble tomorrow."

"You seem to have all the instincts of an Apache," Iron Horse said.

"I take that as a compliment," Clint said.

"That was how I meant it."

"I've had to depend on my instincts and wit my whole life," Clint said. "Someday they'll probably fail me, but not today or tomorrow."

"I hope you are right," Iron Horse said. "I want White Horse's killer so bad I can taste it."

"How close were you?" Clint asked.

"He was my cousin," Iron Horse replied. "I still have not notified his family. Before I do that, I want to be able to tell them I avenged his death."

"So you want vengeance," Clint said, "not justice."

Iron Horse stared at Clint over his coffee cup.

"I think they are one and the same."

"The law might see it differently," Clint commented.

"As long as I wear this badge, I am the law," Iron Horse said.

"That's true," Clint said, "but my agreement was to help you bring this killer to justice."

Iron Horse stared at Clint.

"You agreed to keep me alive until I catch the killer," he said, "If you have changed your mind . . ."

"Too late for that," Clint said, interrupting him. "I've taken a hand in this game, and I have to play it out."

"Maybe," Iron Horse said, "we would be better off not talking so much."

"You might be right," Clint said. He picked up the deck of cards that was on the desk. "Sleep, or poker?"

"Poker," the Apache lawman said, and Clint dealt.

***

They played poker for hours, and then Clint turned in while Iron Horse stood watch. When Clint woke it was still dark. He found Iron Horse sitting at his desk, playing solitaire.

"You better get some sleep," he suggested.

"You are probably right," Iron Horse said. "Must be alert tomorrow." He stood. "I have not heard a thing all night."

"Just the same," Clint said, "better to sleep right under the cot, against the wall, so it'll be hard to get a shot at you from the window."

"Good idea."

"Good night," Iron Horse said. "I'll be up at first light."

"Good night."

Iron Horse went into the cellblock, while Clint poured himself a cup of coffee and sat behind the man's desk. Idly, he started looking in the drawers. He found a stack of wanted posters, took them out and began going through them, just to have something to do.

***

The young Indian girl was dozing next to him, lying naked on her stomach. Blaisdell knew men who enjoyed

135

brutalizing women. He preferred treating them gently, stroking their smooth skin, making love to them slowly, lovingly, while his mind worked on his problem.

Now he sat with his back against the bedpost, one hand stroking her beautiful butt, the other holding a cigarette. At moments like this, life seemed too precious to take chances. No matter how good he was with a gun, there was a chance the Gunsmith could outdraw and kill him. So it seemed foolish to plan on facing him. Since Spotted dog planned on ambushing the sheriff, Blaisdell decided to do the same to the Gunsmith.

The girl stirred, turned her head and looked at him.

"I must go," she said, "unless . . ."

"No, no," he said, patting her on the rump, "we're finished. Your money is on that dresser."

She got out of bed, reclaimed her blanket and wrapped it around her lovely body. He wondered if she'd be walking the street that way, or if she had clothing somewhere else in the building?

She took her money from the dresser and, clutching it in her hand, went to the door.

"Tomorrow night?" she asked him.

"I don't think so," he said. "One way or another, I hope this will all be over by then."

She shrugged and left.

Chapter Thirty-One

By first light Clint had found nothing interesting in Iron Horse's desk. There were some faces on wanted posters that he recognized, but had no reason to think any of them were in the area.

Iron Horse came out of the cellblock, stretching.

"Anything?" he asked.

"Not a sound," Clint said. "There's fresh coffee on the stove."

"Thank you."

The Apache lawman poured himself some, and then sat across from Clint, who was still at the man's desk. Neither seemed to mind the switch in positions.

"Any ideas for today other than sitting out front, making targets of ourselves?" Iron Horse asked.

"Not one," Clint said, "unless you just want to leave that badge on the desk and ride out."

"That is not likely," Iron Horse replied.

"Just thought I'd ask," Clint said. "I guess we should take our chairs out and have a seat."

And they proceeded to do so, each carrying a chair in one hand and a coffee cup in the other.

***

Blaisdell stared out the window of his room, which overlooked the main street. He could see the front of the jail, where the sheriff and Clint Adams were sitting, drinking coffee. He had a clear shot with his rifle, but that wasn't the plan.

He got dressed and went down to the saloon, where he found Spotted Dog, Pete and Lee in the private room. Nettles had arranged for them to have breakfast there.

"More eggs and ham over there, Boss," Pete said, waving to a table that had been set up in a corner.

"Right."

Blaisdell filled a plate, got a cup of coffee and joined the others at the table.

"You fellas sleep okay?" he asked Pete and Lee.

"I guess," Lee said.

"Sometimes it's hard to sleep without a whore's nice firm butt pressed up against ya," Pete said.

Blaisdell remembered the little Indian girl's butt pressed up against him and said, "Well, when this is over you can have all the whores you want."

"Then let's get it over with," Pete said.

"That's what we're gonna do," Blaisdell said. "You two are gonna flush Adams and the sheriff out into the street, where Spotted Dog and me'll take 'em."

"We don't hafta face the Gunsmith?" Lee asked.

"Nope," Blaisdell said, "just flush 'im out."

The two men looked at each other and Pete said, "We can do that."

"Yeah, you can," Blaisdell said, "but this is how . . ."

***

After Pete and Lee left, Spotted Dog just waited for Blaisdell to speak.

"You'll wait for them to get the sheriff out into the street, and then take 'im any way you want."

Spotted Dog nodded.

"I'll take care of Adams," Blaisdell said.

Spotted Dog nodded again, and the two men continued to eat.

***

"There was something I spotted during the night that I didn't mention," Clint said, after they had sat a while.

"What was that?"

"You mentioned something about you and Little Deer. Were you and she—"

"We talked," Iron Horse said, "and spent some time together, but not what you are thinking. Why?"

"I saw her last night."

"Where?"

"I was looking out the window and saw her come out of The Nebraska."

"We closed the saloons."

"I know."

Iron Horse frowned.

"What was she doing there?"

"I don't know," Clint said, "but she had a blanket wrapped around her, and she was . . . well, sneaking."

"I do not like the sound of this," Iron Horse said. "Big Man would be furious."

"That's what I was thinking," Clint said. "But she's got nothing to do with what we're doing."

"Perhaps not," Iron Horse said, "but I will address this matter later."

"I thought you might."

"I do not understand what she could have been doing there," Iron Horse said.

Clint could only think of one reason a woman would be visiting a saloon late at night, but he kept it to himself, for the moment.

Chapter Thirty-Two

"What are you doing here?" Mayor Dandridge asked Nettles. "Did anyone see you come in?"

"I came in the back way."

"Why?"

Nettles walked to the window and looked out. He could see the sheriff and Clint Adams sitting in front of the office.

"I believe something's going to happen today," Nettles said. "Your window has the best view of the street."

"So you arranged it for today?"

"It better happen today," Nettles said. "I plan on reopening tomorrow."

Dandridge got up from his desk and joined Nettles at the window.

"How long will we have to stand here?" he asked.

"I don't know," Nettles said. "Do you have any coffee?"

***

Pete and Lee went out the back door of the saloon, and then through the alley that ran alongside it. When they came to the mouth of the alley, they looked out and across the street. Adams and the lawman were still seated.

"We should get them in a crossfire," Pete said.

"We're only supposed to flush them out," Lee reminded him.

"And we will," Pete said, "but imagine if we were the ones who killed the Gunsmith?"

"I'll go back up this alley and work my way to the other side."

"When I fire," Pete said, "they'll duck for cover, away from me and right towards you."

Lee nodded, said, "Gimme ten minutes," and rushed up the alley.

Pete peered out at Clint Adams and the sheriff, again.

***

"This degree of silence in a town is eerie," Clint said.

"Even for this town," Iron Horse agreed.

Clint scanned the street, his eyes coming to a stop on the window of the Mayor's office. He saw two men before they ducked back.

"Well," Clint said, "the mayor and Mr. Nettles seem very interested in the street."

Iron Horse looked at the window, saw no one.

"Are you sure?"

"They were there," Clint said, "ducked back in a hurry."

"Then they are expecting something to happen, aren't they?" the sheriff said.

"I suppose so."

"I'll keep my eyes left," Clint said.

"I will take the right."

They settled back in their chairs, eyes and muscles alert.

***

"Where were you last night?" Big Man asked Little Deer.

"I was in bed, Papa."

"No, you were not," her father said. "I checked on you at midnight."

"Midnight?" she said, not taking her eyes from the stove. "Oh, at midnight I was taking a walk."

"Where?"

"Just around town."

He glared at her.

"If I find out you were with a man—"

"What man, Papa?" she asked, looking at him. "What would I be doing with a man?"

"That is what I want to know," Big Man told her.

"You are just being silly, Daddy," she said, looking away, again. She knew he hated when she called him "Daddy."

"Am I?" Big Man asked. "Sometimes I think you are just like your mother, the . . ."

She looked at him quickly.

"My mother, the . . . what?"

"Whore!" he snapped. "Your mother the whore!"

Now she grew angry.

"When I have enough money, I am leaving this town, and you!"

"And how are you making this money?" he asked. "Tips from our customers?"

"That is my business!" she said.

They heard the front door open.

"We have a customer," she said to him.

He glared at her again, then turned and stalked from the kitchen.

She had been waiting a long time to get away. She was tired of hearing her father saying nasty things about her mother. Last night's visit with the man, Blaisdell, gave her almost enough money to make her escape, and finally get away from her father, this town, and this kitchen.

Chapter Thirty-Three

Clint and Iron Horse left the bodies of Pete and Lee in the alley. It hadn't taken them long at all to dispatch them. They headed directly to the mayor's office. When they burst in, they found Dandridge and Nettles there. They were still peering out the window, trying to figure out what was going on.

"Wha—" the mayor started, but that was as far as he got.

"Two of your hired guns are dead," Iron Horse said, "and we know a third is Spotted Dog."

"Who is the fourth," Clint said.

"I don't know what—" Nettles started.

Iron Horse cut him off by coming across the room and grabbing the front of his jacket. He stuck a knife right under the saloon owner's nose.

"You are starting to offend the Apache in me," he growled, poking the man's nose with the tip of his blade. "If you don't start talking, I will begin by cutting off your nose, then your ears—"

"All right, all right!" Nettles snapped, trying to slap Iron Horse's hands away. "It was his idea, anyway." He pointed at the mayor.

"What?" Dandridge gasped. "He's lying. This whole thing was his idea."

"What whole thing?" Clint asked.

"Getting rid of the sheriff now that he'd done his job," Dandridge said. "Changing the name of the town, too."

"Who had the idea of killing White Horse?" Iron Horse asked.

"That wasn't supposed to happen!" Nettles snapped. "That was Spotted Dog and . . ."

"And who?" Clint asked.

Nettles licked his lips, but when Iron Horse pricked the tip of his nose and brought forth some blood, he blurted, "Blaisdell."

"Hank Blaisdell?" Clint said.

"You know him?" Iron Horse asked.

"Henry Blaisdell hires his gun out to the highest bidder," Clint said.

"And I know Spotted Dog," Iron Horse said. "He has been a renegade his whole life." He turned to Nettles and prodded him with the knife, again. "Where are they?"

"They have rooms on the second floor of The Nebraska," Nettles said.

"All right," Iron Horse said, releasing the man. "Let's go."

"Where?" the mayor asked.

"You're both going to jail," Clint said. "And then we'll take care of Blaisdell and Spotted Dog."

"You can't put me in jail," Dandridge said, "I'm the mayor!"

Iron Horse gritted his teeth at the man and said, "Watch me."

***

The jailhouse was on the way to The Nebraska. Clint and Iron Horse quickly shoved the two men into cells and ran across to the saloon.

They forced the front door and ran upstairs. After kicking in all the doors to the rooms, they determined that Blaisdell and Spotted Dog were gone.

"The livery stable," Iron Horse said. "We must see if they claimed their horses."

They ran back downstairs, but before leaving Clint said, "Let's check the office."

"Why?"

"I have a feeling."

The two of them went to Nettles' office and entered. It was a shambles.

"Blaisdell searched this place before he left."

"For what?" Iron Horse asked.

147

"Money," Clint said. "He probably didn't get his whole fee from Nettles."

"If he found any money, he is gone," Iron Horse said.

"Okay," Clint said, "*now* the stable."

***

When they got to the stable Leo, the hostler, told them the two men had come in and claimed their horses.

"But separately," he added.

"What?" Clint said.

"Yeah, first the Indian came in and grabbed his spotted pony," Leo said. "Then a while later the other feller came and got his Morgan."

"Did either of them say where he was going?" Clint asked.

"No, not a word," Leo said. "They were in a hurry, and I'm surprised either of them paid me."

"Show me the stalls where their horses were."

Leo took Iron Horse to the stalls. The Apache studied the hoof prints left by the horses, then said to Clint, "We'll have to track them."

"Let's do it, then," Clint said. "They can't have got far."

Chapter Thirty-Four

When they got outside—the sheriff on his horse, Clint on another borrowed mount—Clint said, "Before we leave town . . ."

"Yes?" Iron Horse asked.

"I told you I saw Little Deer outside the saloon last night," Clint reminded him.

"Yes?"

"Maybe she knows something."

"You think she was there seeing . . . who? Spotted Dog?"

"What do you think?" Clint asked. "You know her."

Iron Horse hesitated.

"What is it?"

"Little Deer wants to get away from here," Iron Horse said.

"With you?"

"That never came up," he said. "But she told me when she had enough money she was leaving."

"And how was she making that money?" Clint asked.

Iron Horse looked at him.

"I suppose we better ask her."

***

They reined in their horses in front of Big Man's place and went inside.

"We are closed!" Big Man snapped.

"We are not here to eat," Iron Horse said. "Is Little Deer here?"

"Why?"

"We have some questions."

"About what?"

"We'd better talk to her," Clint said.

"Get out!" Big Man said, balling his hands in fists, menacingly.

"Stop being silly Papa," Little Deer said from the kitchen door.

"You go to your room!" Big Man snapped at her.

She laughed at him and folded her arms.

"That hasn't worked for years, Daddy."

"Don't call me—"

"You gentlemen better come in here," Little Deer said, and backed into the kitchen.

Eyeing Big Man warily, they both walked past him to the kitchen. Little Deer was waiting, arms still folded.

"What can I do for you?"

"Answer a few questions," Clint said.

"About what?"

"What were you doing in The Nebraska late last night?" Clint asked.

She studied the two men, then unfolded her arms and said, "I was visiting someone."

"Who?"

"A friend of Mr. Nettles," she said. "His name was Blaisdell."

"Visiting?" Iron Horse asked. "To do what?"

"Have sex."

"You slept with him?" Iron Horse asked.

"Yes."

"For money?" Clint asked.

"Oh, yes." She looked at Iron Horse. "Are you shocked?"

He glared at her. "Yes."

"But you are not," she said to Clint.

"No," Clint said. "Look, I don't care who you have sex with, or why. But Blaisdell's a hired killer. One of his men—Spotted Dog—killed White Horse. We want them both. Did Blaisdell say anything about where he was going when he left here?"

"You wouldn't think he would," she said. "But he was a very gentle man in bed, and he talked. The whole time, he talked."

"About what?" Clint asked.

"About what he did, and why," she said. "About Spotted Dog being the only man he trusted."

"I don't care about any of that," Clint said. "Did he talk about where he was going? Where he was going to meet Spotted Dog?"

"As a matter of fact," she said, "he did."

***

Spotted Dog rode until he came to a fork in the road. There he dismounted, and while he didn't actually make camp, he did build a fire. That done, he settled down to wait.

***

Blaisdell found some money in Nettles' desk. It didn't amount to his fee, but then he didn't have to pay any of it to Pete and Lee. There was enough there for him and Spotted Dog.

He went to the livery for his horse, saw that Spotted Dog's pony was already gone. He paid the hostler, saddled his horse and rode out of town, leaving Nettles and his friend, the mayor, to deal with Iron Horse and the Gunsmith themselves. After all, there was no element of surprise left for him to use.

He knew Spotted Dog would be waiting for him, and when they met up, they would move on to their next job. Facing the Gunsmith would have to come another day.

Chapter Thirty-Five

Clint had complete faith in the Apache lawman's ability to read sign and track. He got them to a fork in the road about five miles outside of town.

"They stopped here for a short time, just to meet," Iron Horse said, pointing from astride his horse, "then split up. Blaisdell went that way, and Spotted Dog that way."

"Then I guess we're splitting up," Clint said. "You want Spotted Dog, right?"

"Oh, yes," Iron Horse said. He looked down at his chest. "What I don't want is this badge." He took it off and tossed it into the dirt.

"So after you settle up with Spotted Dog, you're not going back to Hellcat?"

"No," Iron Horse said, "never."

"What about your prisoners?"

"The town can do what they want with them," Iron Horse said. "They will probably let them out and go on with business as usual."

"Well," Clint said, "I have to go back for my horse."

"As far as I'm concerned, Clint, you did what you said you would do," Iron Horse said. "You kept me alive. You can go back, get your horse and go on your way."

"What about Blaisdell?"

"It is Spotted Dog I want," Iron Horse said. "I don't care about Blaisdell. I thank you for your help."

Iron Horse urged his horse into a gallop and rode after Spotted Dog. That left Clint with a decision. He certainly would go back to town for his horse, but after that would he move on, or pursue Blaisdell? That was a decision he was going to have to make. And while he was making it, he thought he should probably take the badge back to town, as well.

He dismounted, dug the badge up out of the dirt and put it in his shirt pocket. Then he mounted his borrowed horse and headed back to town.

***

Clint turned the horse in to Leo at the livery, saddled his Tobiano and walked him out.

"Take it easy on him a day or two, and he should be fine," Leo said. "But I wish you'd leave 'im here a little longer."

"Once I put this town behind me, I'll stop somewhere and rest him."

"What about the sheriff?"

Clint took the badge from his pocket and showed it to the hostler.

"He's not the sheriff, anymore," he said. "You mind if I leave this with you?"

"Why don't you drop it off at the office?" Leo suggested. "I don't want it."

"Fine."

Clint walked Toby to the sheriff's office and tied him off outside. Then he went inside to leave the badge on the desk.

"Hey, somebody there?" he heard the mayor shout from the cellblock.

"We're back here! Anybody?" Nettles added.

Clint decided to go back and talk to them.

"You're back!" Nettles said. "Let us out of here, Adams."

"I can't," Clint said. "I'm not the sheriff."

"Then get the sheriff to let us out," the mayor said. "He can't do this to me."

"Well, that's a problem," Clint said. "See, he's not the sheriff anymore. He sent the badge back."

"What?" the mayor said. "Well, where is he?"

"He's tracking down Spotted Dog."

"Then . . . who's the sheriff?" Nettles asked.

"As far as I know, you don't have one," Clint said.

"Then who can let us out?" Nettles asked.

"Beats me," Clint said. "I'm leaving town."

"B-but . . . you can't just leave us here," the mayor said.

"But you got what you wanted," Clint said. "Iron Horse is gone."

"Well, yes, but . . . we're locked in here," Dandridge complained.

"That's your problem," Clint said, and headed for the door.

"Wait!" the mayor shouted. "The job's yours. You can be the sheriff and let us out."

"I don't want the job," Clint said. "In six months you'll be looking to get rid of me. You better hire somebody else."

"We will," Dandridge said. "Just let us out of here, and we will."

"Sorry," Clint said, "like I said, I can't do that. I'm not the law."

"B-but . . . nobody's the law!" Dandridge shouted, as Clint left the cellblock.

"Like I said," Clint called back, "that's not my problem. Adios!"

He left the office with the two men still shouting. Iron Horse was probably right. Somebody would let them out, and they would go back to business as usual.

But that didn't concern him.

Chapter Thirty-Six

Dallas, Tx
3 months later . . .

Clint rolled over in bed to kiss Gloria Dennison's ass.

Gloria was asleep, so Clint ran his tongue along the cleft between her ass cheeks, then kissed each firm, smooth globe tenderly. Gloria moaned and came awake slowly, then more quickly as Clint did other things with his tongue.

Moaning loudly, now, she rolled onto her back and spread her legs wide for him. Clint dove between them and went to work with his mouth and tongue until Gloria was holding back a scream . . .

***

This was Clint and Gloria's third night together since Clint had arrived in Dallas, Texas. He never expected to find her still there, still attending the theater, but when they saw each other across a crowded lobby, they left the theater and hurried to Clint's hotel room.

"You sure do spend a lot of time on my bottom," Gloria said, breathlessly.

"That's because you told me it's too big," Clint said. "I'm showing you there's nothing wrong with it."

"Well, I hope the time you spend on it is better for you than time spent in the theater."

"A million times better," he said.

She snuggled close to him with her head on his shoulder.

"Three nights together," she said. "Where are you off to next?"

"Like I said the last time we were together," Clint said. "Nowhere in particular."

"And when do you intend to leave and head nowhere in particular?"

"I've already been here longer than I thought I would," he admitted.

"I'm taking a train to San Francisco tomorrow morning," she told him.

"And what's in San Francisco?" he asked. Then, before she could speak, he added, "Don't tell me, more theater."

"The best theater in the country," she said. "I have my orders to go there." She ran her hand down over his belly. "You could come with me."

"I could," he said.

"But will you?"

"Maybe," he said.

She moved her hand lower and grasped him.

"Maybe I can change that maybe," she said.

***

The next morning Clint was meeting Gloria at the train station. She had managed to convince him to join her, promising that all expenses would be paid by her newspaper. That wasn't what convinced him, but it was icing on the cake.

He was waiting for her on the platform when he saw a familiar face at the other end. It was Henry Blaisdell. When Clint left Hellcat, he had decided not to pursue Blaisdell. It wasn't his job. But here was the man, big as life, waiting to board the same train.

Clint walked the length of the platform and said, "Blaisdell."

The man turned and looked surprised when he saw the Gunsmith.

"Sonofabitch!" he said. "You been trackin' me all this way from Hellcat?"

"As a matter of fact, I haven't," Clint said. "This is a coincidence."

"Really?" Blaisdell asked. "I hate coincidences."

"So do I," Clint said, "but here we are."

"So, now what?" Blaisdell asked. "You ain't wearin' a badge, are ya?"

"No."

"Then we ain't got any business with each other," Blaisdell said. "And I know you ain't ridin' with that Apache lawman, Iron Horse."

"Oh?" Clint said. "How do you know that?"

"Because he's dead."

"What?"

Blaisdell nodded.

"He made the mistake of trackin' Spotted Dog, and Dog killed him."

"How?"

"What's it matter?"

"It matters," Clint said. "How?"

"Well," Blaisdell said, "if I remember correctly, the same way he killed that other Indian, White Horse."

"Shot him in the back?"

Blaisdell smiled.

"That's a Spotted Dog specialty."

"Where is he now?" Clint said. "Where's Spotted Dog?"

"Well," Blaisdell said, "last I heard he was in El Paso."

"Not San Francisco?" Clint asked.

"Oh, you think I'm goin' to Frisco to meet up with him?" Blaisdell asked. "No, we split up. We ain't partners no more."

"Is that so?"

"We had a fallin' out over money," Blaisdell said. "I'm lucky that savage didn't backshoot me."

"El Paso, huh?"

"You goin' after him?" Blaisdell asked. "Revenge for Iron Horse?"

"It's a thought," Clint said, "but first there's you to take care of."

"Me? I thought we didn't have any business?"

"Well," Clint said, "if Iron Horse is dead, I blame you as much as Spotted Dog."

"That's crazy."

"Maybe it is," Clint said, "but that's how I see it."

Blaisdell spread his legs, squaring himself, evenly balanced. People on the platform read the body language of both men and ran for cover.

"I guess I knew it would come to this, eventually," Blaisdell said.

Clint didn't answer, he just waited for the man's body to give him away. It could be a twitch of the eye, or a shoulder, or a switch in weight. In the end it was none of those things. When Blaisdell went for his gun, it was in a blaze of movement. The man was fast . . . just not fast enough.

As he fell to the platform, face first, Clint turned and saw Gloria approaching.

"I guess you're not going to San Francisco," she said.

"I guess not."

Chapter Thirty-Seven

El Paso, Tx

Clint rode into El Paso on his Tobiano, who was now fully recovered from his injury. El Paso had two sides, American and Mexican, with a bridge between them. He had no way of knowing which side Spotted Dog might be on, if he was still there, at all. If he wasn't, Clint was going to have to find a trail to follow.

He had been thinking about Iron Horse all the way from Dallas to El Paso. Though an Apache, the man had become somewhat citified while in the East. He then returned to the West and paid the ultimate price. There was nothing citified about Spotted Dog. He was still very much an Indian, and apparently Iron Horse had been no match for him.

He boarded his horse and got a room on the American side. Then he decided to give the local law a try. He had never seen Spotted Dog, but he remembered what Iron Horse said the man looked like: tall, flat-cheeks, grey eyes, spots on his face.

He entered the sheriff's office and identified himself.

"I'm Sheriff Dan Fortune. What's the Gunsmith doin' in El Paso?" the lawman asked. He was medium height, in his fifties, and seemed very bored.

"I'm looking for a man, a Comanche named Spotted Dog," Clint said.

"To kill 'im?"

"Well . . . possibly," Clint said. "It seems he killed a friend of mine."

"Here?"

"I don't know if it happened here, or he came here afterwards," Clint admitted.

"What's he look like?"

Clint described Spotted Dog as best he could.

"Well," the sheriff said, "I can tell you he's not here now."

"Was he here?"

"Not that I know of," Fortune said. "I don't recall seein' a man fittin' that description during my rounds."

"What about the other side?"

"Well, I wouldn't know that," Fortune said. "I don't go over the bridge."

"Do you know the sheriff there?"

"Hector Lugo," Fortune said. "He has many other names, but those two are the ones I know."

"I'll have to go and see him then."

"Bring money."

"Money?"

"Sheriff Lugo sells everythin'," Fortune said. "His time, especially."

"I see. Well, thanks for your time."

"Which side of the bridge will you be stayin' on tonight?" Sheriff Fortune asked.

"I already got a hotel room on this side."

"I see," Fortune said. "Well, I hope you'll do you're killin' on the other side."

"I'll do my best," Clint promised and left the office.

The bridge to the Mexican side was walking distance. It was a cracked, stone bridge, and once on the other side you were in Mexico. The law was different there.

While Mexicans and gringos mixed on both sides of the bridge, on the American side the gringos outnumbered the Mexicans. On the Mexican side, it was the opposite. As Clint came off the bridge, the Mexicans looked him over. He expected to be challenged, but it didn't happen. Not yet, anyway.

He continued to walk, past shops, cantinas and restaurants, until he spotted the sheriff's office. It was smaller than the office on the American side. He approached the front door, knocked on it, and entered.

"Señor?" the man behind the desk said. "I can help you?"

"Are you Sheriff Lugo?"

"Sheriff Hector Luis Delgado y Las Truces Lugo, at your service."

The man stood to execute a short bow, which was easy for him, as he was a short man, barely five-foot-five. That done, he sat back down again and asked, "What may I do for you?"

Chapter Thirty-Eight

"I arrived today looking for a Comanche named Spotted Dog." He decided not to give his name unless the man asked.

"Spotted Dog," Sheriff Lugo said. "I know him, Señor. He comes to this side of the bridge quite often."

"And to get here he must pass through the American side."

"But of course," Lugo said, "that is, if he is comin' from the United States."

"Then Sheriff Fortune would be lying if he said he didn't know him."

"Possibly," Lugo said. "That would depend on whether or not Spotted Dog stops on that side. Usually, he comes straight here."

"I see," Clint said. "And would he be here now?"

"If he was here," Lugo said, "I would know it."

"So he's not here at the moment?"

"That would be information," Lugo said.

"Yes, it would."

Lugo stared at Clint.

"Ah, yes," Clint said. "Information."

He took some money out of his pocket and set it down on the man's desk. Lugo looked at the money, then raised his eyebrows at Clint, who set another couple of bills down. Lugo smiled and picked them up.

"No, Señor, he is not here, now," Lugo said. "But he was, and he will be back."

"How do you know?"

"Because he always comes back."

"Well," Clint said, "when was he here and where did he go?"

Lugo raised his eyebrows again. Clint laid some money down and the lawman picked it up and pocketed it.

"He was here a few days ago," Lugo said. "He left to go to San Jose del Alamo."

"Where's that?"

"South of here."

"Why does he go there?"

"He has a wife, there," Lugo said. "But he cannot stand to be around her for very long, so he will be back."

"When?"

"A matter of days."

Clint wondered if he should head for San Jose del Alamo.

"If you try to go there," Lugo said, as if reading his mind, "you might miss each other. If you really want to see Spotted Dog, Señor, you would be better off waiting here. But on the other side of the bridge."

"Why the other side?"

"Trust me, Señor," Lugo said. "That is where you belong. And when Spotted Dog comes back here, he will have to go across the bridge to get to the United States."

"So all I'd have to do is sit by the bridge and wait."

"Si."

"For days."

"Si," Lugo said, happily.

Clint nodded.

"Well, thank you, Sheriff."

"Por nada, Señor."

Clint left quickly before Sheriff Lugo could ask for his name. The man seemed to know a lot about Spotted Dog. Clint suspected they were friends, and when he told Spotted Dog somebody was looking for him, he didn't want his name mentioned.

And he had no intention of sitting by the bridge, waiting for Spotted Dog to come over. He was going to have to find himself another vantage point. For that he might need some help.

***

Clint went back across the bridge and picked out a likely looking cantina. There were some gringos out front, drinking beer, and as Clint entered, he saw that most of the customers were American, as was the bartender.

There were two girls working the floor. They were Mexican.

"A table, Señor?" one asked him.

"*Por favor*," he said. "In the back."

"Si, Señor."

She lead him to a back table and he said, "*Cerveza*."

"Si, Señor," she said. "One beer."

She went off and came back carrying an icy mug of beer.

"Tell me," he said, "are there any men here from the United States looking for work?"

"Si, Señor," she said. "Many men."

"Would you pass the word that I'm looking for someone to do a job."

"What kind of job, Señor?"

"When I pick my man, I'll tell him what the job is," he replied.

"Oh, si, Señor," she said. "I will, as you say, pass the word."

He sat there for an hour and two beers without anyone approaching him. Finally, one man carrying an empty beer mug of his own came over. He was tall, thin, in his thirties, and had a ready smile.

"I hear you've got work for somebody," the man said.

"Have a seat," Clint said, "and we can talk about it."

Chapter Thirty-Nine

Clint waved at the girl for two more beers, and she hurried over with them.

"*Gracias*," he said.

"You speak Spanish?" the man asked.

"I can say beer and thanks," Clint said.

The man laughed.

"Me, too. So, who are ya?"

"My name's Clint Adams," Clint said. "What's yours?"

"I'm Leon," the man said. "Leon Monty. Wait." The color drained from the man's face. "Clint Adams . . . the Gunsmith?"

"That's right."

"Oh . . ." Leon started, getting to his feet.

"Sit down and drink your beer," Clint said.

The man sat.

"I, uh, you're not gonna kill me, are ya?"

"Why would I do that?"

"Well . . . you're the Gunsmith. Ain't that what you do?" Leon asked.

"No, it's not," Clint said. "Is there a reason someone would want to kill you? Are you hiding out down here?"

"Well . . ."

"If you're hiding, you'll need money," Clint went on.

"That's true."

"I've got a job I need done," Clint said. "You're the only fella in here to step up."

"These fellas in here? They ain't lookin' for work. They just wanna drink and whore."

"No whores for you?"

"When I can afford one."

"Well, do this job for me, and you'll be able to afford more than one."

Leon seemed to calm down. He sipped his beer and asked, "What's the job?"

"I'm looking for a man," Clint said. "I want you to help me."

"Who are you lookin' for?"

"His name's Spotted Dog," Clint said. "He's a Comanche."

"Oh, hey—" Leon started to get up, again.

"Sit down, Leon."

Leon sat, but once again he looked uncomfortable.

"Spotted Dog is crazy!" he said.

"You know him?"

"Everybody down here knows him, on both sides of the bridge."

"Does he have friends here?"

"Not one," Leon said. "Everybody's afraid of him."

"That's good," Clint said. "When I find him, it'll be one against one."

"What do ya need me for?"

"I don't want Spotted Dog to know I'm the one looking for him."

"Who'd tell 'im?"

"Sheriff Lugo."

"They're not friends," Leon said, "but you're right, Lugo's afraid of him. So, he'll tell 'im."

"Well," Clint said, "Lugo doesn't know who I am, so he'll just be telling Spotted Dog that somebody's looking for him."

"So if he doesn't know it's the Gunsmith looking for him, he won't be worried."

"Right."

"But I still don't know what you want me to do?"

"I just want you to tell me when Spotted Dog's in town."

"What makes you think he's comin' here?"

"Lugo told me," Clint said. "And remember, he doesn't know who I am. So he figured Spotted Dog's going to kill me. He suggested I sit by the bridge and wait for Spotted Dog to walk over."

"But you don't wanna do that," Leon said.

"No," Clint said, "I want you to do it."

"What?" Leon said. "Me?"

"Does Spotted Dog know you?"

"I don't see why he would," Leon said. "He's a scary sonofabitch and I stay away from him."

"Well," Clint said, "that's pretty much all I want you to do. When you see him, stay away from him and let me know he's here. I'll do the rest."

"And you'll pay me?"

"Handsomely."

"How handsomely?"

"We'll come to a mutual agreement," Clint said. "Are you hungry?"

"Starvin'."

"Then let's eat and talk about it," Clint said.

"Okay," Leon said, "but not here. I know a place with real good food."

"Then lead the way."

Clint paid his bill and followed Leon outside.

"And it's all on you, right?" Leon asked.

"Right," Clint said. "Food, beer, everything, all on me. As long as you do the job I'm asking you to do."

Chapter Forty

Over a supper of burritos and beans, Clint made Leon an offer that the man agreed on.

"And all I have to do is look for Spotted Dog and tell you when he's in town."

"That's right," Clint said. "It's easy."

"You know everybody on both sides of the bridge is afraid of that Comanche."

"You told me that," Clint said, "and I can believe it."

"Why do you want him?" Leon asked.

"He killed a friend of mine," Clint said. "I want to take him back to stand trial."

"You ain't a lawman," Leon said. "Why don't you just kill 'im?"

"What eventually happens will be up to him," Clint said.

"When do you expect him back here?"

"Days, maybe longer."

"And I get paid by the day?"

"You do."

"Well then," Leon said, picking up his beer mug, "let's hope for weeks."

***

After supper they walked to the base of the bridge of the United States side. Across the way were a couple of doorways, including one to a cantina.

"Pick a place to watch from," Clint said, pointing.

"I could lean against the wall right here with my hat pulled down over my eyes and nobody would think twice about me. They'd think I was taking a siesta."

"And if your hat's over your eyes, how would you see Spotted Dog?"

"Well—"

"And are you sure you *wouldn't* fall asleep?"

"Well—"

"Pick a doorway," Clint said.

"Yeah, okay."

"But not the cantina," Clint went on. "It looks kind of busy."

"It is," Leon said. "It's popular with Americans and Mexicans."

"Fine, one of the other doorways, then."

"I'll sit in the doorway of the woodworker," Leon said. "Nobody ever goes there."

"Why not?"

"He specializes in crucifixes and rosary beads."

"Okay," Clint said, "that's your spot."

Sheriff Iron Horse

***

Clint told Leon what hotel he would be at. He had passed it on his way in, and now went and got himself a room. He boarded the Tobiano at a nearby stable.

He could have watched the bridge himself from a doorway, but he didn't want to take a chance that some-one might recognize him. If he didn't get Spotted Dog here in El Paso, who knew how long it would take him to find the Comanche? This seemed the better way to go.

His hotel had a small cantina attached. Unlike American cafes, which tended to have large windows in front, this place had a very small window. So against his standing rule, Clint chose a table in the front, so he could look out the window, fairly certain that no one looking in could see him.

"Señor?"

Clint saw a young girl standing next to his table.

"I can get you something?" she asked.

"*Cerveza, por favor*," he said.

"*Ahora Mismo.*"

She hurried away and returned with a cold beer. To Clint's eye the glass looked fairly clean, so he took it and sipped.

Around him men were eating and drinking. There was a mix of Americans and Mexicans, mostly sitting in groups of twos or threes, with an occasional one seated alone, as he was. For the most part they ignored him, although he noticed one American, and two Mexicans who seemed interested. He split his time between watching them and peering out the window.

He was putting a lot of faith in Leon, a man he didn't know anything about. If he saw Spotted Dog walking or riding past, he'd know that faith was misplaced.

He was on his second beer when he noticed Sheriff Fortune enter the cantina. It was getting dark, so it was possible the man was just making his rounds. But when he saw Clint, he didn't look surprised. As he walked to Clint's table, several of the other tables emptied.

An older woman who looked like the young one came over, as well. She put her hands on her hips and spoke as the sheriff sat.

"Señor Sheriff, you are emptying my place again."

"I'm sorry, Juanita," Fortune said. "Bring us two beers, will ya?"

"Si," Juanita said, shaking her head, "two *free* beers."

Chapter Forty-One

"What brings you here, Sheriff?" Clint asked.

"After you left, I started thinkin'," Fortune said. "To tell you the truth, havin' you walk into my office made me . . . nervous. But to tell you the truth, Spotted Dog makes me more nervous. See, you're a legend. But Spotted Dog is a madman."

Juanita came over with two cold beers.

"Thanks, Juanita."

"Just drink them fast and go," she said. "My customers don't like to drink with a lawman."

"She doesn't like you," Clint said.

"She doesn't like anyone with a badge," Fortune said.

"So, what came to mind after I left your office, Sheriff?" Clint asked.

"I told you," Fortune said. "Spotted Dog is crazy. I thought I needed to make you understand that."

"I think I knew he was dangerous already, Sheriff, but thanks."

"Not just dangerous," Fortune said, "he's out of his mind."

"I'll make sure to remember that," Clint said.

Fortune drank half his beer.

"What about Sheriff Lugo?" Fortune asked. "Did you see him?"

"I did," Clint said. "Paid him for a few nuggets of information."

"You asked him about Spotted Dog?"

"I did."

"What did he say?"

Clint relayed the information Lugo gave him about the Comanche.

"Did he tell you they were friends?"

"No," Clint said. "As a matter of fact, he told me they weren't friends."

"That's a lie," Fortune said. "Lugo may be Spotted Dog's only friend on either side of the bridge."

"I see."

"He's liable to tell Spotted Dog you're lookin' for him," Fortune said. "You'd better be careful."

"He didn't ask me for my name, and I didn't give it to him. So, all he'll be able to tell Spotted Dog is that someone is looking for him."

"That's good, then," Fortune said. "But you'd be better off finding Spotted Dog before he talks to Lugo."

Clint frowned.

"I'll need to be on that side of the bridge, then," Clint said.

"That will be hard to do without being seen," Fortune said. "You'll need help."

"You have somebody in mind?"

"As a matter of fact, I do," Fortune said. "He's not exactly a trustworthy sort—unless you pay him enough."

"Does this fella know Spotted Dog?"

"He knows everybody," Fortune said. "Have you hired any other help, yet?"

"Just a fellow on this side of the bridge," Clint said. "He's just . . . watching."

"Who is it?"

"I'd rather not say."

"Probably smart," Fortune said. "Are you staying in this hotel?"

"I am."

"I can have the man I have in mind meet you here late tonight, just before Juanita closes."

"Will Juanita know him?"

"Everybody in El Paso knows him," Fortune said. "That's why it won't be unusual for him to be seen on the Mexico side."

"So what's this fella's name?"

"He's called Nino," Fortune said.

"That's his name?"

"That's what everybody calls him," Fortune said.

"And how much is Nino going to cost me?"

"Well," Fortune said, "that's gonna be between you and him."

"And what will you tell him?"

"Just to meet you here tonight," Fortune said.

"Not my name?"

"That'll be up to you, also," Fortune finished his beer and stood up. "I'll go and arrange for him to be here tonight."

"You know where to find him?"

"I'll have to locate him," the sheriff admitted, "but it won't be hard. I know what he likes—whiskey and women."

"Just women?"

"Well . . . whores. I'll get to it. As for the beer . . ."

"I'll handle it," Clint said.

"Thanks," Fortune said, and left.

As soon as he was gone, Juanita came over to claim his empty glass.

"Since you are a guest here, Señor, I will tell you, do not trust that man," she said, keeping her voice low.

"But he's the law."

"He uses that badge to hide behind," she said. "He is not a good lawman."

"Gracias, Juanita," Clint said. "I'll keep that in mind."

"More cerveza?"

"Yes, please," Clint said. "And bring a drink for yourself. We have something to talk about."

Chapter Forty-Two

Clint was sitting in the empty cantina later that night, waiting for Sheriff Fortune's Nino to appear. When there was a knock on the door, Juanita went to answer it. She unlocked it and allowed a man to enter.

"Señor," she said to Clint, "Nino is here."

"Thanks, Juanita," Clint said. "You can go to bed now."

"*Gracias, Señor.*"

Nino was a short man, but strongly built, with muscles bulging beneath his shirt. He approached Clint while smiling and revealing several gold teeth.

"Señor," he said, "Sheriff Fortune says you have work for me?"

"Have a seat, Nino," Clint said. "You want a beer?" He pushed a full mug across the table to him.

"*Gracias, Señor.*" Nino drank thirstily, emptying half the mug while Clint took stock. The man wore two guns in a bandolier that crisscrossed his chest, and two knives on either side of his belt.

"What can I do for you, Señor?"

"You know a man named Spotted Dog?"

"Si," Nino said. "A very bad hombre."

"I'm looking for him," Clint said, "and I need some assistance across the border."

"*Si, Señor*," Nino said, "you should not go over the border alone. You want me to accompany you?"

"I want you to go there and watch for Spotted Dog to arrive in town."

"And what will the Señor do when he does arrive?" Nino asked. "Kill him?"

"That'll be up to him," Clint said.

"But Señor," Nino said, "you are a man who kills people, no?"

"Sheriff Fortune said he wouldn't tell you my name."

"Oh, si, Señor," Nino said," he did not tell me. But he said you are a *muy hombre malo*, also."

"I see," Clint said. "Let me get you another beer."

He stood up, walked around behind the bar to draw another beer for Nino. When both his hands were occupied, Nino stood and drew his gun.

"I do not need another beer, Señor Gunsmith."

"So the sheriff did give you my name?"

"Yes, he did. Now, por favor, remove your gun from your holster and lay it on the bar."

Clint started to reach for his gun.

"Left-handed, please," Nino said.

He took his gun from his holster with his left hand and put it on the bar.

"*Bien.* Now slide the gun all the way to the end of the bar so that it falls to the floor."

Clint slid his Peacemaker so it fell off the bar to the floor.

"*Muy bien,*" Nino said, spreading his arms expansively so that his gun was no longer pointing directly at Clint. "Now I have the Gunsmith at my mercy?"

"Do you?" Clint asked. He brought the shotgun up from beneath the bar, and pointed it at Nino.

"*Madre de dios,*" Nino said, "where did that come from?"

"Juanita, the owner, left it there for me."

"*Perra!*"

"Now you either drop your gun, or I'll blow you in two."

Nino, looking amused, shrugged.

"I have been paid to kill you, Señor," he said. "I cannot do that if I drop my gun. And that shotgun has probably been under that bar for a very long time. It most likely not fire, or it will certainly blow up in your hands."

"No, it won't."

"How can you be so sure?"

"Because I cleaned it before I let Juanita put it beneath the bar."

The smile dropped from Nino's face.

"You lie."

"One way to find out"

Nino frowned.

"Drop your gun to the floor and I'll let you walk out. Tell Sheriff Fortune it didn't work."

"Easy, Señor," Nino said. "Here, see?" He dropped his gun. "I will leave now."

He turned to go to the door, but as he did, he drew his other gun left handed, intending to shoot Clint across his body. But Clint was ahead of him. The shotgun boomed. It was a single barrel weapon, but there was enough buckshot to toss Nino across the room, where he fell to the floor in a bloody heap.

Juanita came out from the back.

"We need to get this body out of here, Juanita," he said. "I don't want the sheriff to know what happened. Not yet, anyway."

"*Si, Señor*," she said. "I will get my brothers to take him away."

"And thanks for this," Clint said, setting the shotgun down on the bar.

"It was my pleasure, Señor," she said. "Anything to cause Sheriff Fortune much trouble."

"Oh, well," Clint said, "you've done that."

Chapter Forty-Three

Clint woke the next morning lying next to Juanita in her bed. He suspected someone might try for him during the night, so he asked her if she had another room.

"I have just the one, Señor," she said, with a smile.

She was a full-bodied, lusty woman in her forties, and her energy in bed was boundless.

"You are looking at me," she said, opening her eyes.

"I am," Clint said. "You're a helluva woman."

She rolled onto her back, her full breasts leaning to either side.

"I am an old, fat cantina owner and mother, and I am trying to build a life for my daughter."

"Your daughter?"

"She works in the cantina," she said. "Her name is Gisella." She pronounced it "Gee-sella," with a 'G' as in "God."

"Well," Clint said, "you may be a cantina owner and mother, but you're certainly not an old, fat—"

"That is enough," she said, reaching out to grab his cock. "Do not tell me I am not old, show me."

He rolled toward her and said, "With pleasure."

***

"What did your brothers do with Nino's body?" he asked later, as they dressed.

"Do not worry," she said. "They can bring him back whenever you like."

"I'm trying to figure out what to do with him," Clint said. "Might take a few days."

"That is fine." She ran a comb through her mane of hair and looked at herself in the mirror. "*Jesus Cristo*, there was a time when I was as beautiful as Gisella."

He walked up behind her and put his arms around her waist.

"You're still beautiful."

"You only say that because I let you use my shotgun."

"Well, there is that." He kissed her neck. "If the sheriff comes around asking questions, you don't know anything."

"I was not even awake," she said.

"Right."

"Come," she said. "I will have Gisella make you a big breakfast."

"That's good," he said, "because somehow, I built up an appetite last night."

***

In the cantina Clint sat, this time at a back table. He now realized that Spotted Dog probably had two friends in El Paso, each wearing a badge. That meant that Fortune had probably told Lugo who he was.

"Señor?" Gisella said, stopping by his table. She had an amused look on her lovely face.

"Gisella."

"An American breakfast, or Mexican?"

"If I'm not insulting you," he said, "American."

"Mama said to give the man anything he wants," the girl said. "American, coming up."

Clint watched her walk away, and remembered what Juanita said about once being that beautiful. He hoped Gisella was able to look at her mother and see that she would still be beautiful years from now.

It seemed to only take minutes, and Gisella was back with a plate of steak-and-eggs, and black coffee, then went back to the kitchen and returned with a basket of biscuits. He was halfway through wolfing it down when Sheriff Fortune appeared at the door.

" 'morin'," the lawman said. "Mind if I sit?"

"Not at all," Clint said. "Have some coffee."

Gisella brought a cup for the sheriff.

"So?" Fortune said.

"So what?"

"What happened with Nino?" Fortune asked. "Was he able to help?"

"I don't know," Clint said. "He never showed up."

"What?"

"I waited here for hours," Clint said. "I finally went to bed."

"He didn't show up?" Fortune asked.

"Nope."

"Are you sure?"

Clint stopped eating and looked across the table at the lawman.

"I think I would have noticed," Clint said.

"A short, squat, hard lookin' little Mexican," Fortune asked.

"Nobody showed up, Sheriff," Clint said. "I was sitting here for the longest time. Not a soul. Sorry. I guess he didn't want a job."

Clint saw the confusion on Sheriff Fortune's face.

"Okay, yeah, that was probably it." He stood up. "Sorry I couldn't help."

The man turned and hurriedly left the cantina. He was going to go looking for Nino. Clint decided to help him find him.

Juanita came over.

"Is there anything I can do?"

"Yes, as a matter of fact," Clint said. "I think I figured out what I want your brothers to do with Nino's body."

***

Later in the day Sheriff Fortune returned to his office. As he entered, he stopped short when he saw Nino's body propped behind his desk. He walked to it, just to be sure, and saw the wound in the man's chest.

He sat in a chair in front of his desk and stared at the man's mutilated body. He was sure Clint Adams had killed Nino. That meant the man knew that Fortune had sent Nino to kill him. Which also meant the Gunsmith would come for him. He had to get in touch with Sheriff Lugo and let him know what happened. Lugo was then going to have to make sure Spotted Dog knew that Clint Adams was waiting for him.

They were going to have to make sure Spotted Dog killed the Gunsmith before the man could kill all three of them.

Chapter Forty-Four

Clint walked to the bridge, saw Leon standing in his chosen doorway—or rather, sitting there. He looked completely relaxed, lounging beneath a wide-brimmed sombrero.

Clint walked over and said, "Lose the hat."

Leon looked at him.

"I thought it made me blend in."

"Stand out, you mean," Clint said. "That hat's not for you."

Leon frowned but removed the sombrero and put his own hat back on.

"Better," Clint said. "Leon, you know a man named Nino?"

"Everybody here knows Nino," Leon said. "He does odd jobs."

"Like killing people?"

"Among other things," Leon said. "Why?"

"He came to see me last night."

"That's bad."

"It was bad for him."

"You killed him?"

"I did," Clint said. "He left me no choice."

"If Nino tried to kill you, somebody put him up to it," Leon said.

"It was the sheriff, Fortune," Clint said.

"Jesus, the law?" Leon's surprise seemed to be disingenuous.

"You knew all along the sheriff was crooked, didn't you?" Clint asked.

"To tell you the truth, I believe all lawmen are crooked."

"So the same goes for Sheriff Lugo."

"You met him," Leon said.

"So, both lawmen will be covering for Spotted Dog."

"I expect so."

"I think I'm going to have to change my plans," Clint said.

"How're you gonna do that?"

Clint pointed.

"Give me that sombrero," he said.

***

Clint crossed the bridge on foot, wearing the sombrero and sapped in a green serape. He tried to slouch, so as not to give away his true height. He slowly walked to the sheriff's office. He figured by now Sheriff Fortune had told Sheriff Lugo what had happened. Clint needed to get to Lugo without being recognized. He didn't want the man to be warned.

When he reached Lugo's office, he sat on the board-walk in front, appearing for all intents and purposes to be lazily languishing there. He didn't expect what happened next, but it worked to his advantage. He planned on entering the sheriff's office, but the door opened, and Lugo stepped out.

"Hey, you, *cabrón*," the man snapped, "get away from here."

Clint didn't move. Lugo stepped further out of his office, leaned over and put his hand on Clint's shoulder.

"I tol' you, *stupido*, move!"

Clint brought his gun out from beneath his serape and pointed it at Lugo's face.

"Why don't we both go inside, Sheriff," he suggested.

Lugo looked shocked but turned and reentered his office with Clint behind him.

"What is this about, Señor?" he asked, once the door was closed.

"Sit behind your desk," Clint ordering, grabbing the man's gun from his holster, "hands on top. Do it!"

"What is this about, Señor?" Lugo asked.

"We're going to have a talk," Clint said, pulling a chair over and sitting across from the lawman.

"About what?"

"About you, Sheriff Fortune, and Spotted Dog. And, oh yeah, a fella named Nino."

Sheriff Lugo looked unhappy.

Chapter Forty-Five

"I do not understand, Señor," Sheriff Lugo said.

"Nino's dead, Lugo," Clint said. "You know that, right? Sheriff Fortune sent him to kill me, but it ended up being the other way around."

"Sheriff Fortune?" Lugo said, aghast. "*Madre de dios*, he did that?"

"Don't play dumb, Sheriff," Clint said. "I know you and Fortune are friends with Spotted Dog. I want that Comanche, and I don't want the two of you getting in my way."

"Me?" the man said, his eyes wide. "*Amigos* with that . . . savage?"

"I'm not buying your innocent act, Lugo," Clint said.

Lugo dropped his innocent expression and frowned at Clint.

"What is it you want me to do, Señor?" he asked.

"That's easy," Clint said. "I want you and Sheriff Fortune to go fishing."

"Señor?" Lugo looked confused. "Fishing?"

"And don't come back until I've dealt with Spotted Dog."

"But, Señor, I cannot just leave town. I am *el jefe*."

"That's fine," Clint said. "Then I'll just put you in one of your own cells until I'm done."

"Señor, you are threatening not one, but two representatives of the law."

"That's just what I'm doing." Clint confirmed. "And Fortune is lucky that I don't just kill him for sending Nino after me."

Lugo suddenly decided to fend for himself.

"I had nothing to do with that, Señor," he assured Clint.

"I'll take your word for that, Sheriff," Clint said. "You go across the bridge, round up Sheriff Fortune and then find yourselves a fishing hole."

"But Señor . . . when should we come back?"

"Give it a few days," Clint said. "Who knows? It could all be over by then."

"Señor—"

"I'm assuming you know who I am."

"Si, Señor—"

"Then you know I mean what I say."

"Si, Señor."

"Then off you go, Sheriff."

The man reached for his gun.

"Uh-uh," Clint said. "No gun. Just go."

"Si, Señor."

Lugo got to his feet and hurried out the door. Clint stepped outside to make sure he went over the bridge. Then he pulled a chair over to the front door and, covered by the sombrero and serape, sat and waited.

***

Hopefully, there was no access to a telegraph for the two lawmen to send Spotted Dog a message. That was, if they had not already sent him one. There was certainly a possibility the Comanche would bypass El Paso and reenter the United States another way. Clint could only hope he wasn't wasting his time.

He sat for hours, wondering what the two sheriffs were doing. Hopefully, they were sitting side-by-side at a nearby fishing hole.

***

When Sheriff Lugo appeared at Sheriff Fortune's desk and told him his story, the American said, "I don't plan on going up against the Gunsmith."

"Neither do I," Lugo said.

"Spotted Dog is gonna hafta face him all by himself."

"If he survives, he just might come after us, next," the Mexican pointed out.

"Then we'll just hafta hope he doesn't survive the Gunsmith," Fortune said.

Chapter Forty-Six

The El Paso street got very quiet and reminded Clint of his time in Hellcat. Word had obviously gotten around that trouble was brewing. And if it was this quiet, maybe the time was very soon.

Clint was getting very hot beneath the serape and sombrero. He decided Spotted Dog must know by now what he was riding into. Whether he recognized Clint or not didn't matter. He tossed the sombrero away, then slipped the serape off and set it aside. The tension he felt in the air was thick with energy. Then he heard the sound of an approaching horse, just a slow clip-clop-clip. If it was the Comanche he was taking his sweet time riding in. Clint stood and moved to the end of the boardwalk. He had the sheriff's office to his back, so there was no access for a backshooter.

He looked down the street, waiting for horse and rider to appear, but when the horse finally came into view, it was riderless. Now he knew the Comanche was in town and was ready for him.

He ducked back as the riderless pony went by and waited. Soon, Spotted Dog himself seemed to appear on

Clint's right, standing and staring at him from the end of the boardwalk.

"Are you alone?" Clint asked.

The Comanche carried a rifle and wore several knives. He could have been anywhere between forty and sixty years old.

"You shot White Horse and Iron Horse in the back," Clint said. "Why would you face me now?"

"I just saw my wife," Spotted Dog said, shrugging. "She makes me wish I was dead."

Clint laughed.

"So you want me to kill you and save you from your wife?" Clint asked. "Why don't you just kill her?"

"A man should not kill his own wife," Spotted Dog said.

"You could have someone do it."

The man's stone-faced expression never changed.

"So, you'll just stand there and let me kill you?"

As his answer, Spotted Dog suddenly moved to his left and disappeared.

"I guess not," Clint said.

He ran to the end of the boardwalk and looked down the alley Spotted Dog had just darted into. It was empty. He started down the alley slowly, but there was no other access until he reached the end. Rather than leading to the rear of some buildings, it led to another street.

"Come on, Spotted Dog," he called out. "Are you going to make me go all through town to find you?"

No answer, then suddenly he was there again, across the street.

"Damn, how do you do that?" Clint asked. "You move like a ghost."

Spotted Dog jerked and suddenly a knife was flying toward Clint. Clint barely had time to move before the knife imbedded itself in the wall next to him.

"You could have killed me—" he started, but Spotted Dog was gone. "So we're playing a game."

No answer.

Clint crossed the street to where Spotted Dog had been standing. The Comanche's movements were uncanny. Clint was glad they weren't out on the trail, where the man would be more at home.

Something here in town was going to give him away when he stepped out. A creak of a board or the sound of a rifle—if he ever intended to use his rifle. He would run out of knives to throw, eventually.

Clint stood stock still and listened. It was deadly quiet, so any rustle could be heard if he listened hard enough. He may not have been a Comanche, but his instincts had kept him alive this long.

So he waited . . .

Sheriff Iron Horse

***

Spotted Dog knew he had one more chance with a knife, and then he would have to use his rifle. He wasn't sure he could outshoot the Gunsmith. As much as he hated his wife and never wanted to see her again, he could not just let the man kill him. Maybe, when this was all over, he *would* kill his awful wife.

He stood with his back to a wall, waiting for a time to step out and end this . . .

***

Clint remained stock still. He knew Spotted Dog was doing the same. What he had to do was <u>hear</u> where he was coming from next. And there were only so many choices, because the Comanche would be outside, not inside a building or on a roof.

Spotted Dog was wearing moccasins, but while his movements made no sound, his weight on the boardwalk did.

Clint turned, drew and as the Comanche stepped into view, already bringing up his rifle, Clint fired.

The bullet struck the Comanche in the chest, driving him back so that his foot slipped off the walk, and he went tumbling to the dirt.

Clint walked to the fallen man, kicked his rifle away, and bent to check him. His eyes were open, staring at the sky, but he was dead. He straightened and looked around. No one had come to see what the shooting was about.

Clint Adams was done with El Paso, and with incidents that had started it all in the Texas town of Hellcat. Hopefully, from whatever heaven or happy hunting ground Iron Horse was in, he was satisfied.

Upcoming New Release

THE GUNSMITH
J.R. ROBERTS

THE RED LADY OF SAN FRANCISCO
BOOK 478

**For more information
visit:** \underline{\text{www.SpeakingVolumes.us}}

On Sale Now!

THE GUNSMITH
BOOKS 430 – 476

**For more information
visit:**

Upcoming New Release

LADY GUNSMITH
J.R. ROBERTS

ROXY DOYLE AND
THE QUEEN OF THE PASTEBOARDS
BOOK 10

Coming Soon!

**For more information
visit**: www.SpeakingVolumes.us

On Sale Now!

LADY GUNSMITH
BOOKS 1 - 9
ROXY DOYLE AND THE LADY
EXECUTIONER

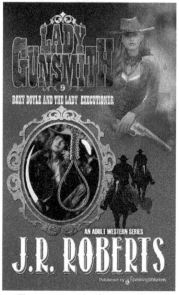

For more information
visit: www.SpeakingVolumes.us

On Sale Now!

TALBOT ROPER NOVELS
ROBERT J. RANDISI

**For more information
visit: www.SpeakingVolumes.us**

On Sale Now!

AWARD-WINNING AUTHOR
ROBERT J. RANDISI (J.R. ROBERTS)

**For more information
visit:** <u>www.SpeakingVolumes.us</u>

Sign up for free and bargain books

Join the Speaking Volumes mailing list

Text

ILOVEBOOKS

to 22828 to get started.

Message and data rates may apply.

Printed in the USA
CPSIA information can be obtained
at www.ICGtesting.com
LVHW041604011023
758229LV00033B/301

9 781645 407522